The
Anthropologists

White on White

Walking on the Ceiling

The Anthropologists

Ayşegül Savaş

SCRIBNER

LONDON NEW YORK SYDNEY TORONTO NEW DELHI

First published in the United States by Bloomsbury Publishing Inc, 2024

First published in Great Britain by Scribner, an imprint of
Simon & Schuster UK Ltd, 2024

Copyright © Ayşegül Savaş, 2024

The right of Ayşegül Savaş to be identified as author
of this work has been asserted in accordance with the
Copyright, Designs and Patents Act, 1988.

5 7 9 10 8 6 4

Simon & Schuster UK Ltd 1st Floor
222 Gray's Inn Road London WC1X 8HB

Simon & Schuster: Celebrating 100 Years of Publishing in 2024

Simon & Schuster Australia, Sydney
Simon & Schuster India, New Delhi

www.simonandschuster.co.uk
www.simonandschuster.com.au
www.simonandschuster.co.in

The authorised representative in the EEA is Simon & Schuster Netherlands BV,
Herculesplein 96, 3584 AA Utrecht, Netherlands. info@simonandschuster.nl

A CIP catalogue record for this book is available from the British Library

Trade Paperback ISBN: 978-1-3985-2990-8
eBook ISBN: 978-1-3985-2991-5
Audio ISBN: 978-1-3985-2992-2

Printed and Bound in the UK using 100% Renewable Electricity
at CPI Group (UK) Ltd

For Maks and for my grandfather

Beginnings and Endings

In a moment of panic, we decided to look for a home. We'd been in the city for several years by then, and from time to time we worried that we weren't living by the correct set of rules, that we should be making our lives sturdy. I worried more than Manu did, but he often acquiesced to my apprehensions.

Cosmology

For many years, it had been just the two of us. When we met, the world expanded and it also contracted: it stretched large enough for the two of us—a whole universe—and it left everything else behind a curtain.

We were so young then, barely out of childhood. On weekends, we'd walk off the university campus to spend the day in town, among older people whose lives seemed at once real and unreal. Real, because that was how we imagined actual life in the abstract; unreal, because it did not seem we would ever be like them.

We went to the town bookshop, to the coffee shop, to the record store, even if neither of us knew anything about the type of music sold there: cool and stylish and, to us, exotic.

We were scholarship students in a foreign country, which is to say that we recognized something in each other. We'd been raised by similar types of people—their worries, their discipline, their affection, their means—even though we had grown up on opposite ends of the world. We accepted, children that we were, that we would remain foreigners for the rest of our lives, wherever we lived, and we were delighted by the prospect. Back then, it didn't seem to us that we'd ever need anyone else, in our small world that was also a universe.

Rough Drafts

We'd arrived in the city on a whim. We had lived in small towns after university, and the city seemed alluring; the start of something else. We had an idea that we would live in other places afterward. For a while, we wouldn't worry about making things sturdy.

We found an apartment for rent on an unremarkable street, in an unremarkable part of town, and we decided on it without much thought. Back then, we were only playing out our adulthoods rather than committing to them.

Our apartment was small and a little dark, the kitchen not much more than a sink and stove. But we loved it all the same, and for a reason we didn't clearly articulate, we stayed in the city. Instead of the framed posters we'd had since university, we hung paintings we'd bought at the flea market: a plate of fruits, a port scene at sunset. We liked the paintings, yes, but we also liked what they might mean about us—people with real paintings on their walls.

We had a routine; we grew fond of it. Perhaps we were tired of that first rush of excitement in a new setting, and the gradual draining away of color.

Now it was time to expand. *To make a life*, as some people called it. We wouldn't have called it that, but we agreed that we had to make things a bit more solid.

Daily Life

Manu left home early to go to work at the nonprofit organization on the other side of the city. While he made breakfast, I made a pot of coffee and sat with him at the table in pajamas. It was a ritual of sorts, sitting across from each other, face-to-face. There were few rituals to our lives, certainly none that carried any history, at least not the history of traditions, of nations and faiths. So these small things mattered. I would make sure to sit with him at the table.

Before he left, we kissed in the hallway.

Okay, Manu said, back in my shoes.

Afterward, I lay on the couch and read. I made tea once the coffeepot was empty.

I had just received a grant to make a documentary, though the funding was flexible enough that I could use it for many other things. We wouldn't need to worry about paying rent for the coming year. The money we saved would help toward a down payment for a small apartment. We had a little more, a wedding present from our parents, though their earnings were modest and the currencies of our native countries were constantly losing value. Still, they considered it their duty; and they were sad, they said, that they couldn't afford to give us more.

Whenever I introduced myself as a documentary maker, people assumed that I was a sort of journalist, that I was drawn to investigation. This hadn't been my impulse when I started filming years ago, when I recorded my parents and grandparents, walks around our neighborhood, late-night conversations. Back then it was just an itch, something I did without thinking very hard about it. I didn't worry about the outcome, what to do with the hours of footage I accumulated, about giving shape to anything. I put together bits and pieces to show Manu, stitching together scenes in our particular humor, our shared logic. There was a film about my mother, or rather, about my mother's wardrobe. Another about the grocer in the neighborhood where I'd grown up, from the vantage point of the owner's father, who sat all day at the shop. Now that these seemed to me like the work of another person, I could say that they were good films: joyful and naïve. For later projects I traveled to countries I knew little about. I filmed a school for refugee children; a group of migrant women running a soup kitchen from a bus. Sometimes, I believed that making a documentary was a process of empathy, an education. Other times, I thought bitterly that this was simply what documentarians wanted to believe, leaving their subjects as soon as they accumulated the necessary footage. Still, these films taken together gave a sense of social critique, and it was for this reason that I had received the grant, allowing me freedom for the first time in my career.

For now, I knew little beyond the fact that I wanted to film daily life, and to praise its unremarkable grace. I didn't want to travel anywhere, to investigate the ways of other places, but to remain in the city, and establish some rules.

Future Selves

During our first weeks of searching, we viewed an apartment that was even smaller than ours but impeccably restored, with an open kitchen fitted tastefully and resourcefully, and a bathroom that gave the feeling of being in a luxurious setting.

Each time we visited a place for sale, we were intrigued by all the different lives happening in the city, the arrangement of space to work and rest, to store and display; the priorities of strangers that were so different from our own.

The owner was a flamboyant man in his fifties, whose exquisite belongings seemed to have been bought to fit the shelves of his home. After showing us in, he took his place on a leather armchair and let us walk through the apartment ourselves, aware that it needed no explanation. Afterward, we sat at the café down the street, with a red lacquered façade and marble tables. If we were to live there, we said, we'd come to this café for lunch and late-night drinks, would know the waiters by name. The thought was pleasing though somewhat foreign, as if we'd put on very expensive clothing that didn't belong to us.

A few days after seeing the apartment, we met up with our friend Ravi at a bar in our neighborhood. We met there whenever we thought we'd have a quick drink, and almost always ended up ordering the platter of fried onions and sweet potatoes and mozzarella sticks, which made us feel sick a few hours later.

We sat at the bar drinking pints of lager and showed Ravi pictures of the apartment from the real estate website. In the photographs, the apartment looked even more like a museum.

Ravi took the phone from Manu. He zoomed in on the round window above a reading nook.

Damn, he said. The Royal Navy.

He then said that it seemed ideal for a couple who received no guests and had no children. That part, he added, was something for us to decide.

So you like it? I asked.

Sure, he said, it's great. I mean, it is what it is.

Ravi was always throwing things out there, not quite committing to them, not quite letting us know what he really thought.

Principles of Kinship

We'd met Ravi our first year in the city. We recognized in him something we recognized in each other: the mix of openness and suspicion; a desire to establish rules by which to live, and only a vague idea about what those rules should be.

For a while, Ravi was our only friend in the city, and that suited us well. We would meet up every few days and spend hours doing very little. Sit by the river eating peanuts. Walk the whole city, picking out apartments we'd like to live in. Hang out on a square with a bottle of wine. Ravi and Manu liked coming up with setups for comedy skits. Ravi and I liked to discuss traits that made a person alluring and how to do work that interested us. It wasn't so easy, we said, to know your true passions. Many things seemed appealing on the surface but after a while, they felt oppressive.

For a living, Ravi tutored high school students and also managed online advertisements for a retailer on the other side of the world. It had taken us months to find out how he made money, because he always skirted the topic, perhaps embarrassed that he wasn't doing work he truly loved. It was often the case, for people our age, that an interesting job was tantamount to being an interesting person.

Whenever we went over to Ravi's studio, Manu and I would look through his collection of photographs, posters, old manuals, journals, and textbooks. He found them at flea markets and on the street, always with an idea of ways he would put them to use, though he never did. His true passion was collection, the accumulation of expired things, their foggy poetry.

This stuff is so cool, we always told him. You should really do something with it.

Yeah, Ravi said, I will.

This was the other thing: it seemed that our interests could be legitimized only if we made something of them—a book, an exhibit. We often said what a shame this was; we romanticized artists of past decades, doing work with great joy and creativity without turning it into a product.

Still, we belonged to our own times.

Ways to Live

For the documentary, I considered places that I could get to know with time, places that received outsiders without judgment.

There was the cemetery not far from our home, where we went on walks in the early evenings and befriended the deceased whose names and tombstones appealed to us. There were the city buses with their changing tempers—the leisurely afternoon emptiness, the evening crowds, the late-night drunks. Finally, I settled on a park north of where we lived, which Ravi had introduced us to. It had a different atmosphere to the rest of the city—more relaxed, perhaps, more welcoming. Elsewhere there was a sense of precarity, as if our belonging might dissipate from one day to the next. Ravi felt it, too, I think, but he was not the type of person to express such things, because he had a horror of seeming needy.

A few days after I settled on my topic, Ravi, Manu, and I went to the park for a picnic. It was still warm, too warm for September. We didn't know whether to be delighted or worried. We bought chips and beers. We packed a ball, a blanket, our books. We lounged on the grass all day long, going to the kiosk every few hours to get more beers. We left at closing time, when the guards began whistling from every direction.

I love a good day of rotting, Ravi said.

That's what I wanted to film. The slow and leisurely rot of a day.

Perspective

On the phone, my grandmother asked me if I had planted anything in our window boxes. She always phoned too early, when I was barely out of bed, forgetting about the time difference. She would begin each call with something she had thought of during the night.

If you want, she said, I can get you some seeds and your mother can send them to you by post.

My grandmother had a way of confusing perspectives during conversations, the small and the big, the faraway and close by. She might not know the new developments in our lives—that I had received a grant, that we were looking for an apartment to buy—but she would ask what we'd made for dinner the previous day or whether I had taken down my winter clothes already, with the cooling weather.

It hadn't occurred to me to plant anything in the window boxes. Sometimes I bought potted flowers, which wilted in a matter of weeks. Then I would replace them with other pots, their flowers blooming, their leaves healthy, hoping naïvely each time that they would remain that way.

I asked my grandmother what I should plant. She looked very intently at the screen. My mother had recently bought her a smartphone so that she could call me on video as well, instead of poking her head into the frame whenever my mother and I talked. I was expecting her to say geraniums or roses. My grandmother told me parsley, oregano, and chives.

She went on to list combinations of foods I could eat with the herbs: chives and cheese, parsley and walnuts, oregano and tomatoes, tomatoes and chives and cheese.

Mano will appreciate it, too, she said. She often called Manu different names than his own and I didn't correct her.

What else? my grandmother asked. I told her I was trying to bring my new project into focus, and about our picnic at the park the previous weekend. Daily life, I said, was a difficult story to tell.

Forget about daily life, my grandmother said. No one cares about that.

Moreover, she continued, you should always include a historical episode—the Roman times, for example—so we have an opportunity to learn something new.

What if you only learned something emotionally new?

Asya, my grandmother said, don't complicate the point. We named you after a whole continent and you're filming a park.

I mumbled in agreement, because I didn't want her to think I was strange. This was a fear of mine: that my family would think I was becoming a stranger.

Instead, I told my grandmother I had a photograph of her on my desk. The one of her reading under a tree.

I was sixteen years old, she said. I was the best writer in class. No one could write an essay like I did. And I was awarded a prize for my singing.

She sighed, meaning that she had wasted her life.

The City

Manu and I had lived in other places together. But something about this city reflected the cadences and proportions we wanted from life. Its hours ticked alongside our own; we admired its colors and edges and embellishments, the organization of its neighborhoods. I cannot say that we felt familiar, only that we *wanted* to become familiar, and so we accepted the city's ways.

Besides, we'd always known that wherever we lived would require us to change. There was no place where we could feel at ease, no language that, after so many years, we could sink into like a deep sleep. And we hadn't even begun to consider the greater issues of being rootless yet, such as where we might be buried, what words of which language we might begin to lose when old age chipped at the reserves of our minds.

Natives

Lena was my only native friend in the city. Manu and I were a little embarrassed by the fact that all the people we knew were foreigners, as if this were a judgment about us. When we went to lively plazas, we had the sense of a joyful world evading us. It wasn't as if everyone at the plaza knew one another—people would be gathered in groups of two or three, but it seemed that they were there on greater authority.

I had met Lena at the birthday picnic of a woman named Sharon. She and her husband, Paul, organized a monthly gathering of expatriates, which I went to mostly without Manu, because he objected to the formal pursuit of friendship. Sharon often expressed her dissatisfaction with the city, its snobbery, its reluctance to befriend foreigners. But she also liked to commend herself on her decision to move abroad: the great courage it had taken and the many rewards it brought.

I arrived at the party with a bottle of wine, a log of cheese, and a novel in translation by a writer whose books I'd seen on bookshop displays. There were so many bookshops in the city, beautiful ones crammed with unusual selections. It was difficult for me to read entire novels in the language of this city, and the bookshops, like the sight of crowded plazas, gave me a pang of being left out. Manu was feeling sick, and glad to have a reason to skip. Ravi hadn't come either, in Manu's absence. Whereas I felt that we should make an effort, even if we didn't really like these people.

I placed my present on the stack forming next to Sharon, who looked queenly on a quilt. She was wearing a long coral dress. Sharon's closest friends, three women who organized a wine-tasting club, also wore bright outfits like bridesmaids. One of them was running after Sharon's daughter, Izzy.

We must catch up! Sharon said to me, her attention drifting to the people waiting to greet her. I went to the table to drop off the wine and cheese. It was filled with food: a heaped basket of cherries, pastel-colored pastries, a tray of oysters. I was glad Manu and Ravi weren't there to take offense or be sarcastic. They would claim it was insincere, a show of wealth and taste.

Lena was standing by the table, hands in her pockets, surveying the food. She was tall and spectacularly cool. Her clothes looked just a bit too big for her. I was studying her when she turned to speak to me.

Still life with oysters and cake, she said.

Homo sapiens gathered for ritual, I offered.

Lena didn't switch to English, as natives often did upon hearing my accent, or some error in conjugation.

We talked the entire picnic, relieved not to be socializing with the rest of the group, while trying to decipher people's connections to one another. Lena said that she was embarrassed to have landed at the picnic of someone she didn't even know—she had come along with one of the other guests, who'd abandoned her to join his close friends. But she said it so cheerfully, and I was intoxicated by her clarity.

When the picnic ended, she held out her phone and I tapped in my number. By the time I got home, I had a text from her, proposing to get together in a few days. I thought happily that our life in the city was finally taking shape. But it had been over a year since the picnic and Lena remained my only native friend.

The Foreigners

That's what we called them, though we weren't blind enough to think that we were any closer to the city people. Still, there was something that set the foreigners apart, a confidence with which they claimed their place in the city. Perhaps this was because we'd first encountered the foreigners that Sharon gathered into her fold, all of them groomed and accomplished. As a group, they seemed indistinguishable from one another—in their cheer, their well-rounded lives, the hobbies they tended to like delicate gardens. They talked about their secondary pursuits with modesty and eagerness: amateur marathon runners, potters, rock climbers, opera enthusiasts. It was not quite passion, because they didn't abandon themselves to their enthusiasms, but remained contained at all times.

The foreigners gathered regularly, but were careful not to overstep the rules of the group: the meetings and the friendships didn't evolve in frequency or intimacy. Perhaps this was why we felt foreign to the foreigners— Ravi, Manu, and I—because we were constantly tipping beyond the rules we'd set for ourselves. We would agree to meet for a drink, then stay at the bar all night. We would be determined to see a museum show, then spend all day sitting around. We had no hobbies to speak of, only ideas that we bounced back and forth. And what we wanted above all, what we wanted to find in the city, were people with whom we could abandon the rules even as we were establishing them, those people who could become our family.

Fear of Loneliness

Manu was content not to follow up on friendships he found meaningless. It delighted him to decline invitations and spend the weekend just the two of us, or with Ravi.

Sometimes I reproached him for it.

We have to form a group, I told him. We have to find people we can rely on. I cited studies about dementia and friendship. Old men in small coastal towns who went daily to coffee shops to meet their friends, among whom Alzheimer's was rarer than in urban settings.

That's really interesting, Manu said, noncommittally.

But do you understand what I'm saying?

Yes, he said. Friends are wonderful.

Urban Costume

I thought of Lena as a true native, and I envied this about her. She knew shopkeepers in various neighborhoods, called waiters and bartenders by name in many places she took me to. She held flirtatious banter with them, back and forth, tugging and letting go. This was my problem with the city: I didn't know how to flirt with it. I was too eager, too forward, like a clingy lover.

Whereas Lena found the city oppressive. She thought the people lacked imagination. She loved to say that she would be moving away soon.

I'd live anywhere that's not here, she said, and I felt worried about losing my only native friend. But she had remained in the city, working at a café. It was a job she had grown out of, though I found it charming, its proximity to city life, its utter nativeness. I went weekly to pick her up toward the end of her shift. From there the two of us usually went to an exhibit of Lena's choosing. She was always resentful that she hadn't done anything with her day except dish out hot drinks and pastries. I admired her grudge toward life and her petulant claim on it.

I hadn't yet told her about our apartment search. It seemed like the type of thing Lena might make fun of. She liked to make fun of things she found too ordinary, and I often took her sarcasm to heart. Besides, it might shock her to learn that we had any money to spare for a mortgage, when she lived within the exact confines of her paychecks. But I did tell her that I'd started filming the park.

The park? Lena asked. What about it are you filming?

Just that. A day at the park.

Someone paid you to do that?

I guess so.

You can travel with that money, she said. I can't believe you're going to use it to go to the park every day.

Future Selves

Another place that interested us was a loft built inside an old factory. We took the train east from the city center, out past the suburbs. From the station, we crossed a highway on foot before arriving at an area of industrial lots, some abandoned, some converted into trendy homes for young families, others occupied by immigrants. There was a mosque, and next to it a basketball court. On the evening of our visit, lanky boys were throwing a ball with casual focus, calling out from time to time to their friends passing by. At the entrance of the mosque stood a small man with a thickly furrowed forehead, greeting those arriving for evening prayers.

Inside the gates of the converted factory was another world altogether. The walls were overgrown with green, the plots of adjacent lofts marked with terra-cotta pots and round tables. The owners of the place we were viewing had three children, with toys made exclusively of wood. There were bicycles for each member of the family, stacked against one wall, part of the cheerful clutter that communicated sanity and care. When we arrived, the family was cooking all together, the children standing on stools, chopping and peeling with their small hands. I wondered whether the scene was planned to coincide with our visit, though they were all so merry, and welcomed us so warmly.

The place was spacious enough that we could host guests without having to change our routine. Our families visited us for only a few days at a time, and we made it clear that any longer would be difficult for us. But we were embarrassed to set a limit on our hospitality. We imagined a future when they could stay without constraints, the way it happened back home, when relatives would spend weeks, even months at one another's homes.

Afterward, Manu and I couldn't find a café in the neighborhood to sit and talk about our impressions, so we took the train back.

When we showed the pictures to Ravi that week, he told us he'd take the train to visit us on weekends.

Only if I have to, he added, just because I'm such a good friend.

On the phone Manu's parents asked about the schools in the two neighborhoods, the availability of doctors, especially pediatricians, even though Manu and I had never said we wanted to have children. We'd never denied the possibility, either. It was one of the aspects of our lives we still needed to bring into focus, so that we could better picture a future home. The process was an act of imaginary acrobatics, trying to launch ourselves forward, with only a guess of where we wanted to land.

Gardening

I told my mother on the phone what my grandmother had said about planting herbs.

Your grandmother hasn't sown a single seed in her life, my mother said. I really wonder at her pontificating about your plants.

My grandmother had moved in with my mother after my grandfather passed away, around the same time that my parents separated. At that point, I had been abroad for several years and the new living arrangement shocked me.

When I expressed my surprise to my mother, she asked, Where else do you propose she should live?

But you're still young, I said. You shouldn't be living with your mother.

She can't manage the house by herself.

She can move somewhere smaller.

And in three years?

We'll think about it then, I wanted to say. I told her we could consider a retirement home. In other countries, such an option wouldn't seem so outrageous.

Asya, my mother said, what on earth are you talking about?

I'd adapted too quickly to the idea that autonomy should come above all else. I thought of this as a moral value, an unquestionably desirable state. This was surely the type of thing that would make me strange in the eyes of my family, if not a stranger.

I asked my mother what she thought I should plant.

Well, she said, I suppose it's useful to have fresh herbs on hand.

Neighbors

Tereza lived two floors up from us. She was old in body but not in mind, even though she had begun to stumble over the language she'd spoken for forty years, after she left her own country.

Before we became friends, she would find excuses to ring our doorbell. One time, it was to inform us that we should move our bikes, before work began in the court-yard. Another time she asked if we would like to have the remaining fruit in her fridge, which would go bad while she visited her grandchildren over the weekend. We accepted the fruit. From then on, Tereza would ring the doorbell weekly, with or without an excuse, and we'd invite her in for tea.

She was very small, which was a surprise each time we saw her, as if she had sprung out of a fairytale. She had bright blue eyes and wore theatrical clothes in unex-pected combinations—canvas and silk, velvet and plastic beads. At first I had taken her outfits as a sign of eccen-tricity, or an artistic sensibility, but she was simply childish. She delighted in life.

Tereza's daughter lived outside the city with her husband and children. The family visited infrequently and Tereza went to see them whenever she was invited— holidays, birthdays, New Year's.

I made a habit of buying a good box of cookies for Tereza's visits, as well as loose-leaf tea—something Manu and I would usually never bother with. I guessed that from Tereza's perspective, our flat must look a little haphazard. Tereza's apartment was grand, with the old-fashioned luxuries of real homes. Plenty of armchairs and blankets, sets of china for different occasions, wicker baskets. Things that could not be bought wholesale, in a hurry. I wanted to understand how such a place came into being, whether the acquisition of any of these objects had been an event in Tereza's life, despite their current look of nonchalance and permanence.

When my grandmother moved in with my mother, an entire home had been disposed of. Among the few reminders of my grandmother's previous life were the silver frames with family photos, the wool blanket with which she draped her knees when watching soap operas, a mother-of-pearl box, the walnut dresser. All these items stood out among their new companions, the sense of time they exuded even denser in their modern surroundings.

From time to time, my grandmother wistfully inventoried the furniture of her former home. If my mother was around, there followed the usual argument:

Why did you give it away, then, if you were just going to beat me on the head about it?

I didn't think you wanted any of it.

Did I ever tell you that?

Well, what's done is done.

★ ★ ★

Tereza didn't care very much about entertaining, even though she brought out silver tongs for pastries and used the small porcelain plates from the buffet rather than the ones in the kitchen. Manu and I had been a little stiff on our first visits, careful about what we did with our limbs, how we held our cups. But we soon relaxed. We pulled up our feet on the sofa, served ourselves from the kitchen. We realized that Tereza didn't keep track of manners; what mattered to her was conversation. Manu and I had no spare sets of plates or matching glasses, but we had plenty of discussion in our lives. For Tereza, ours was a true wealth. She asked us about our friends, our opinions on music and poetry, about the political situations in our countries whose details she never quite retained, beyond the fact that things didn't look very bright. This was Tereza's general disposition: that the world had become a dark place after a brief period of hope in her youth.

Almost at every visit, she recounted the story of how she and her classmates at university had stood all in a line to block the entry of soldiers into the faculty of letters. Her plate remained untouched as she talked, sometimes frantically, trying to tell us as much as possible in the span of a meal. At some point, we had switched from tea to dinner, and we were all happy about this change, our new intimacy.

Tereza wasn't a good cook, though something of her generation elevated her dinners to ritual: bread and butter on the table, relishes, cloth napkins and candles.

The ingredients were of the finest quality, ordered for her weekly by her daughter, from an expensive supermarket with beautiful, unnecessary packaging.

The daughter called every evening, which coincided with our dinners. The landline rang a few times before Tereza decided to answer it. When she returned to the table, we asked if all was well, to which Tereza responded:

She's relieved I haven't died yet.

The first few times she said it, we acted shocked. Then we began to say it with her in chorus.

We agreed that Tereza was a little odd and that she was one of us.

Parallel Lives

On the phone with his brother, Manu was talking about the different neighborhoods we'd been to on our search.

You'll see when you visit, he said, or something like that. I didn't understand everything he was saying, but I could always tell from his tone who he was talking to. It was too enthusiastic, full of effort. He saw me looking at him, and went to the bedroom as if I had glimpsed something embarrassing.

Manu would often tell me about things he and his brother had done as children, their mutual likes and dislikes, their adventures. At university, he would report to his brother all the new and strange things he had witnessed, his sense of loyalty still rooted back home. Around the time that Manu and I graduated and began forming our own mythology, his brother married and, in the following years, had three children.

It didn't happen all at once, though it seemed like it: the brothers diverged fully in their paths. Manu's brother had never been to the cities we'd lived in; he had neither the time nor the means. And although it seemed unlikely now that he ever would, Manu would end his anecdotes by adding, You'll see when you come.

On our visits there, we spent time with Manu's brother's family, entertaining the children for a few hours, giving them presents, always with a sense of guilt that we were hiding something, trying to conceal just how different our own lives were from theirs. The strain I heard in Manu's tone when he talked on the phone was also this: the effort to make it seem that he was still part of their old schoolboy mythology.

Anthropology

The summer of our second year at university, I traveled to Manu's hometown to conduct fieldwork. We'd started dating a few months earlier, and it was unthinkable from then on that we should be apart. The other person was our native country, even if we didn't know a word of each other's mother tongues.

I was studying anthropology and the trip seemed the shortest route to spending the summer together. My fieldwork involved daily bus rides from Manu's parents' apartment to an international organization where I played with the neighborhood children, made tea, and arranged documents. Otherwise, I would sit in the courtyard with the men and women from the neighborhood who came daily to observe the commotion at the center. Manu was doing an internship at the same organization, making charts of the center's expenses, finding ways to show that the community had benefited from donations.

In the evenings, Manu's brother picked us up and drove us to a bar outside town with a bowling alley.

I was supposed to be taking daily notes for my thesis, though I found my subjects self-explanatory, if not a little disappointing. From my handful of anthropology classes, I'd come looking for a list of specimens: kinship structures, gift exchange, rituals, costumes, notions of the sacred and the profane. I should've known better than to expect that these would be performed daily in clean strokes for me to collect. It was just life, in a somewhat ugly town. There were afternoon snacks of Fanta and stale vanilla cake. The children that came to the center wore sneakers and had cell phones. They listened to the same pop songs as the rest of the world.

★   ★   ★

My last year at university, one professor of anthropology trained our attention inward at the close of every lecture. The professor looked wizened beyond age and seemed perpetually troubled by the world, which made me inclined to take her teachings seriously. She asked us to notice that *just life*—writing papers, going to parties, applying to jobs—could always be mapped out following the structures we learned about in class. Friday night blackouts and graduations and hockey games, the cigarettes we bummed off one another outside the library. All these were the unspoken foundations of our society, whose rules we had perfected, so as not to think of them as rules but as the smooth tracks of life. From time to time, the professor would ask us to imagine an anthropologist observing the everyday routines with which we had set up our lives. They might be arbitrary or essential, but they were rules to a game nonetheless, one which gave an illusory sense of harmony and permanence.

The first time she brought up the imaginary anthropologist, I visualized a tiny Martian in a safari outfit, taking notes on a flip chart. But even with the absurd image, the point was clear.

The imaginary anthropologist remained with me after I finished university. I would summon her to narrate the simplest interactions when I tried to untangle the layers of an argument, when I edited footage, when I was dressing up for an event. I called on the anthropologist to examine our lives as we moved from place to place, where we were never natives. What would she write down in her pad if asked to study Manu and me as a tribe of our own? Trained as she was to identify the ways of people rooted in their homes, their language and customs, what would the tiny anthropologist point to in our make-shift apartments, where we lived without a shared native tongue, without religion, without the web of family and its obligations to keep us in place? What would she identify as our rituals and ties of kinship, the symbols that constituted a sense of the sacred and the profane?

Because it often seemed to me that our life was unreal, and I summoned the anthropologist to make it seem otherwise.

Fieldwork

How often do you come to the park?
 Do you have a favorite spot?
 What do you do here?
 What don't you do here?
 Do you have rituals associated with the park?
 Do you have any memories associated with the park?
 Do you recognize any of the park's regulars?
 Do you come here to be alone or to not feel lonely?

Notions of Loyalty

Some months into our apartment search, my father came to visit. He was going to stay at a hotel instead of our spare room. From his previous visits, he must have decided that everything was small in our home: the two-person couch, the cramped shower, the guest bed. I knew the trip would be an expense for him, but at that age, he was used to certain things.

The first morning, I met up with him in front of his hotel. It had rained earlier and I was wearing a trench coat.

Look at you, my father said, you fit right in. I felt embarrassed, as if I'd overdressed. It was the old fear of seeming a stranger to my family.

We had planned on going to a museum, and I took us on a longer path so we could walk the lively shopping street. My father stopped to look at a display window: corduroy trousers, cardigans, fedoras. Handkerchiefs with polka dots. Everything looked dignified. Seeing the price of a coat, my father let out a long whistle.

Motherfuckers, he said. Plain highway robbery.

After the museum, we took a bus to a touristic plaza, because my father believed that a proper visit should include the highlights. I told him that Manu and I never went to these places in our daily lives and that I would like to show him other neighborhoods, but my father ignored my objections. Even after several visits, he didn't really know how we lived: he had never been to the market where we shopped on weekends, the cafés we frequented, the tree-flanked square where we went to read on weekend mornings.

He hadn't met Ravi either: what would they have talked about? My father didn't feel at ease in a foreign language, though he and Manu got on well, pointing and laughing and making a big show of their simple conversations. Manu was never offended when my father switched languages to talk to me.

There was another reason I hadn't introduced my father to Ravi. It was the sense that something might go wrong—that there would be a misunderstanding, or disappointment. I don't mean that I would be embarrassed of my father in front of Ravi. It was the opposite—that my father would be dismissive of our friendship.

My father had many friends in the world. There was, in particular, a group of four men that formed a sort of clan. They went on holidays together, watched football games, played cards, visited each other at sickbeds, borrowed money. One of them had loaned our family a big sum when my parents were buying their first home. We weren't able to pay it back as planned, and yet the friendship didn't suffer. Later, my father had sold his car and given the money to another friend in debt, to my mother's great distress. It was a constant point of tension in their marriage. All this had recently started to seem unusual to me, now that Manu and I were trying to figure out how much we could pay for a mortgage, and whether a bank would even offer us one. But it would never have occurred to us to ask Ravi for help, even if he had the money. It would be freakish; it might mean the end of our friendship. Whereas my father's friends loaned each other big sums as easily as buying a round of drinks, even though none of them were very well-off.

Throughout my childhood, I'd thought of these friends' intimacy as an archetype of friendship. I'd imagined I would have friends of my own, from whom I could ask anything in my adulthood: *people of character*, which was a denomination my father used. Being *without character* was how he damned anyone he found lacking in integrity. What sort of integrity he meant had never been quite clear, though I used to think that it would become obvious with time. And I felt wary of introducing my father to our friends, in case he should say that they lacked character.

In the evenings of my father's visit, after Manu came back from work, we went to restaurants that specialized in meats of various sorts. When his dish arrived before him, my father pointed his fork and knife toward the food, examining it carefully, then cut off a small chunk and ate slowly. He was a big man, with a big appetite, and he usually ate so fast he barely chewed. But abroad, he was decorous.

After dinner we saw him off to his hotel and came home to watch an episode of a detective show, neither too dark nor too cozy, unraveling around the disappearance of an innocent person and the appearance of a kind but troubled detective. We had watched dozens of shows with this exact setup and we started each new one with the same thrill of anticipation, the comfort that good and evil would be delineated.

Afterward, we smoked a joint in bed before turning off the lights.

Do you think he's having a good time? I asked Manu in the dark.

I think so. What do you think?

I hope so.

It was the best we could manage regarding the heartbreak of a parent's visit: that we hadn't tried hard enough, that our lives felt strange to them and that these days of tourism were all we would ever have together.

On the last day of the visit, Manu went to work a few hours late so we could all have breakfast. I hadn't managed to work at all while my father was there; it seemed rude, when I only saw him a few times a year. Still, I was restless to get back to my routine, and felt guilty about my agitation. We went to the grand café with white tablecloths and took a table by the window.

My father asked about my documentary. Somehow, the topic hadn't come up throughout his stay, perhaps because jumping right into important subjects would expose how little we knew about each other's lives. It was always on the last day, over the last meal, that we breezed through the facts.

I told him about my early footage from the park. I added that I was still trying to find my angle.

Why're you filming a park? my father asked. You have to do work that matters to you. This was true, and I didn't have anything to add.

When Manu went to the bathroom, my father brought out an envelope from the inside pocket of his coat and reached for my backpack.

What is that? I said. What're you doing?

New Year's present, my father said, even though the New Year was a few months away.

You don't need to give us a present. Please take it back.

I was too embarrassed to try and stuff the envelope in his pocket. But I had seen from the thickness that it was more than my father could afford.

Couldn't we put this aside for your next trip?

I'm your parent, he said.

Outside the café, Manu hugged my father goodbye.

It's been a very special time, he said. Please come back soon for another visit.

Manu knew that I found it difficult to say simple things like this, so he'd say them for me, too. My father and I had never exchanged formal affirmations of affection: I love you, I love you, too. These were phrases foreigners said, children and parents in films.

Manu walked away in the direction of the metro to go to work and I hailed a taxi for the airport.

You don't need to come, my father said, knowing that I would accompany him anyway. At the terminal, he kissed my cheeks and said I shouldn't wait for him to go through.

It'll be faster for me, he said, with such conviction that I now believed my presence was in fact a nuisance.

In the Park

I always sit here, at the top of the hill. You can see down to the lake, the merry-go-round, and the gates. There's the metro stop, if you look farther. My doctor told me to look out into the distance for my eyes, which are always tired. I don't have a balcony at home, and there is nothing to see from the window except the building across the street. That's not very much for the eyes to roam. I always wanted to live in the countryside, where you can see the horizon, and you can see the sky. But I never have. And I don't think I will. I've never been married, but I have many cats. I will show you a picture. No, I don't bring them to the park. They like it where they are. They're probably all lined up at the window now, looking out.

Fieldwork

We met Ravi in front of his studio and went to the square nearby. We'd brought a bottle; Ravi brought down a corkscrew and glasses. I asked what they would like from the corner store and they said chips, but I bought hummus and tomatoes and nuts anyway, even though Ravi and Manu found it burdensome to have decent foods on a regular hangout.

We sat on the plaza, by the steps of the fountain. Now well into autumn, we had an urge to make the most of the remaining light and mild air.

So, Manu asked, how was everyone's day?

Fine, Ravi said. Nothing to report.

There must be something, Manu said.

Really, nothing.

Well then, what did you have for breakfast? I asked.

Here she goes, Ravi said.

Maybe I'd gotten it from my grandmother. I just wanted to know how people lived—really lived.

During my interviews at the park, I was mesmerized by the routines of strangers: I wanted to ask questions that burrowed deeper into the fabric of a single day. As I continued filming, I was also beginning to articulate a feeling I'd had, dormant, for a long time. Everyone, it seemed to me, had something truly weird about them, something unique and bizarre. This uniqueness was most apparent in everyday acts, in the banal rather than the extraordinary: the way they picked clothes for the day, the things they ate, how they spent a free hour. This was their compass, it seemed to me, more so than any moral abstraction. I told Manu and Ravi my hypothesis.

Well, Ravi said, make sure you don't estrange your subjects with your weird questions.

Manu said that I might be right. And he added, wisely: Different people are different.

Native Tongue

Over the years, Manu and I had taught each other words and phrases from our own languages: those without any equivalent, that defined not just something essential about our mother tongues, but about us as well. These words became part of our shared language, growing in meaning once they were plucked out of their habitats. The native lexicon illuminated aspects of the other person—an orientation toward the world. Though I'd always had a sense of Manu's sensitivity toward shifty behavior, I recognized it once again when he taught me a term that literally meant *stealthy eating*, used to describe people who made plans in private. The moment he explained it to me, I understood Manu's heightened attention to Ravi's last-minute announcements—that he was going on a date, that he had bought a concert ticket for a band we all loved.

So, I asked, could you use this word for Ravi-type behavior?

Absolutely, Manu said.

Sharing our language was a bit like sharing family histories, which we still did, after so many years together.

From time to time, Manu brought up the one about a suitor who had asked for his mother's hand in marriage. This Western man, visiting Manu's hometown, had become very rich in later years; his name was known around the world. His mother had told Manu, only once, that the man had wanted to marry her. Manu's grandfather had said no, and that was that. Manu had never known if his mother loved the man, or whether she was wistful.

She must be, I said, if she told you the story so many years later. Maybe it was her way of saying that she might have had another life; perhaps she shared the story during an unhappy time with your father.

We never allowed our parents their unhappiness, I said, and we never allowed them their individuality, before they were shackled to parenthood.

Let's not get ahead of ourselves, Manu said, in response to my hypothesis.

Child-Rearing

We were at the neighborhood café when a tourist family walked in. The father was carrying one child, the mother another. Everyone seemed to be emerging from a fit of tears. From our table, where we sat drinking wine, we observed them trying to settle down. They had so many things coming out of their backpacks—plastic boxes and tissues and crayons. Little grubby cardigans. Soon enough, there were fries on the floor and more tears.

Oh god, I told Manu. What a nightmare.

What a shit show, Manu said.

This is supposed to be a holiday? I said.

I know, Manu said. Geez.

Then he added, Aren't we smug.

Because he couldn't push this conversation to its meanest heights. He reserved a bit of tenderness for such scenes, for the little humans and the new order they created with their arrival. He was reluctant to dismiss the question, always hovering above us, above our unencumbered days.

Native Tongue

We spoke differently to each other when there was no one around. Something like a high-pitched mumble.

There were years of inside jokes, accumulated personas, and mispronunciations. We had nicknames for each other, words with no meaning in any dictionary. That was how we came to claim our own language, a native union, rather than two people speaking to each other in a foreign tongue.

We would've been self-conscious if anyone heard us speaking like this, like characters in a cartoon. But we weren't embarrassed of each other.

And we had a name for the two of us: the *T*s, short for a word we'd invented more than a decade ago, which signified two people who were in love, who were a little sad, a little misfortunate, who had always been somewhat clumsy and lonely. This was our name for who we were, and it was with great tenderness that we noticed the quality of being a *T* in others, and bestowed on them our own title.

Courtship

I hadn't met up with Lena in a while because she was seeing a man whom she nicknamed the Bulldog. When I texted her for news, she wrote back dismissively that it wasn't worth my time to listen to her boring affair, which I nevertheless took to mean that she was dismissing me rather than the man. I had an idea that Lena had a real life outside of our friendship, one in which she was a native in ways I could never understand. What did Lena and her native friends joke about? Where did they go on a Friday night? What did they consider cool or weird? This last one was always on my mind. Just like the fear of my family thinking me a stranger, I feared that strangers would find me weird.

Once Lena broke up with the Bulldog, I went to her café as usual and waited for her at a back table, writing down some scenes I was planning to film at the park: the cypress grove, the lake at sunrise. I would try to capture some ambient sound. So far, my footage consisted of interviews, and I wanted to give a sense of the backdrop that informed the anecdotes.

When Lena's shift was over, she brought us leftovers from the kitchen: a salad with pomegranate seeds, an onion tart, a bowl of grains with spinach, and a heaping basket of bread.

I started questioning her about the affair, trying to sound nonchalant, while Lena ate with speed. It appeared that spending time with the Bulldog had starved her.

He was boring, she said. He was unbearably boring.

How so?

All he wanted to do was sit around and talk about nothing.

She took a bite of the tart and strings of onions tore off the crust. She said, Don't you have any friends you can set me up with?

Let me think about it, I told her. I was flattered that she asked me, even if I already knew that I didn't know anyone suitable. Lena always made fun of me for spending so much time with the foreigners, whom she said were insufferable. Then there was Ravi, but Manu and I had never met anyone he was involved with. We guessed, from time to time, that he was going on dates, from a fleeting reference or a few days of silence. He never suggested introducing us to anyone, and I had the sense that he was reticent: because of our judgment, perhaps, or the unnecessary tangle this might introduce to our friendship. And perhaps Manu and I preferred it that way: the undivided attention of our friend, the sense of ownership, our trio as an indivisible whole. Besides, I doubted Lena would have enjoyed spending time with Ravi. All we ever did with him was sit around and talk about nothing.

Collective Action

There was another anthropology professor at university who became a controversial figure during our student years. I didn't like this professor very much, perhaps because I hadn't done very well in his class. The professor had spent his entire career studying one remote mountain village. All his work had to do with the various structures of this village, the kinship ties, economy, power dynamics. Then, someone from the village had become very famous with a memoir about the hardships of her people. She had written a heart-wrenching story of poverty and danger, of the government's ignorance of this remote place because its natives were a different ethnicity than those that ruled the country. The woman had drawn considerable attention to this part of the world—more than an anthropologist could ever do. She was on talk shows and radio programs, speaking about the lives of her people. The professor was one of the few foreigners who had ever spent time in this village, and he happened to know that what the woman was saying was not entirely accurate. While the hardships she mentioned were certainly real, the woman herself nevertheless belonged to the village's elite, and hadn't suffered the poverty and injustices she described in her memoir. The semester I was taking his class, he'd written an article unveiling the woman's elaborations and agglomerated accounts.

The situation irritated me. I thought the professor greedy for exposing the woman and petty to detract from the hard-earned attention finally given the remote village. Back then, Manu and I used to argue about this. Manu said it was the professor's responsibility, as an academic, to speak the truth, whatever the consequences. I didn't have a very good counterargument but I still disagreed. And I secretly thought that the woman hadn't done something so terrible, after all, stitching together the stories of her people into a single biography, of which she was the protagonist.

But later, once we settled in the city, I was no longer sure what I thought. It wasn't that I had come to agree with Manu. Rather, I mistrusted the woman's process of abstraction, simply because I'd grown so weary of life in the abstract. For most of the people we were acquainted with, Manu and I were nothing much more than our countries of origin, our accents, our work. And I yearned for a specific existence.

Society and Nature

I left the apartment soon after sunrise and arrived when the mist was still hanging low to the ground. It was the earliest I had seen the park. The late-October colors glowed in the clean light of the day. Birdsong rang out from treetops, ducks glided along the surface of the lake. The runners with cold, firm limbs looked full of focus. So this was what happened here every morning, while I was at home, drinking coffee. Everyone at the park at that hour, people as well as animals, seemed to be part of something—a tribe, a secret gathering. I set up my camera on a tripod and filmed the dewy grass, the silence interrupted by chirps and footfalls. The sound of the city could be heard in the distance.

That evening at dinner, I told Manu that we should make a habit of going to the park in the mornings.

That would be nice, Manu said. Maybe not every morning.

I was always coming up with routines for us, in bursts of panic. One time, I announced that we should be having an array of animal parts in our meals—kidneys, liver, tripe—for all the benefits that our ancestors had reaped and that were foreign to our sterile bodies. Another time I insisted we should tell each other our dreams every morning, to share our subconscious landscapes.

Manu was calmer than I and less prone to thinking something was wrong.

It's great you're enjoying filming, he said.

Identity as Performance

There was a woman we saw around our neighborhood whom we called the Great Dame. She was a filmmaker, as well as a patron saint of dreamers and sidekicks, and had a devout following among those who were themselves not very practical at life. She could portray life with humor and wit. She knew how to convey enchantment.

We saw the Dame some mornings on a café terrace a few blocks from where we lived. She sat in the very front row, her face turned up at the sun, piles of books and newspapers next to her coffee, a plate of bread, butter, and jam. I always slowed my step to take in the details, and I hoped there might be some sort of osmosis, whereby her spirit rubbed off on me.

Other days we saw her at the park, her face once again oriented toward the sun, her trousers rolled up, her limbs splayed across several chairs she'd pulled together to make a throne. The Dame liked the sun, and she liked leisure.

In the evenings, at the same café where she sat earlier with her books and coffee, the Dame would be at the bar drinking a cocktail, and chatting with the people who surrounded her, of which there were quite a few.

Ravi, Manu, and I had once stood at the other end of the bar and shared a pitcher of wine, observing the scene. Manu made a series of snide observations: the Dame's regal air, her constant proximity to her drink, her brusqueness. At one point, she was visibly rude to a man who cut her off.

If you will let me speak, the Dame said slowly, aware that we were all watching her.

She loves it, Manu said. It's all an act.

Ravi and I remained deferential. We admired the Dame's confidence, even her impatience. We said that she must've had enough of people cutting her off, and she would no longer tolerate it.

Why should she? Ravi said.

That's the way to live, I added. But I wasn't so sure. It looked as if the Dame had broken away from everything that constricted her—that stood in the way of her work, her love for life. And yet it seemed that in breaking free altogether, she had no one left besides the group of fawning strangers who got on her nerves.

She had been married and divorced three times. I knew this because Ravi and I had fetched out every item of personal history we could from the internet, and photos of the Dame as a young woman, looking fierce and intelligent, even at the risk of eclipsing her beauty. Years ago, she'd made a documentary about a group of women—artists, cooks, socialites, pigeon-feeders— whom she filmed in their bedrooms and studios and on the street. I loved this film, its humor and stubbornness. The way it didn't smooth out the women's madness. There were scenes of the objects cluttering their homes, slow shots of their thickened hands, their creased faces like lines of a poem. On-screen, the women were restored to a state of dignity that might have been refused them in their lives. I had always thought that the film was a kind of self-portrait, a collage of what the Dame valued in herself and how she wanted to be seen.

Gift Exchange

In some ways, Ravi was also an expert at self-portraiture, or rather representing himself through objects. Most weekends, he went to the flea market at the edge of the city, beginning at the small, barren park, and extending for several kilometers, with smaller stalls set up on the branching streets. He arrived early in the morning, wearing his parka with big pockets, and inside it a vest, also with numerous pockets. By the end of his hunt, they would be filled with sepia photographs; small and heavy objects; wooden, brass, and leather tools; an old notebook or frame. He propped the notebooks on a shelf above his bed, like postcards, alongside the empty picture frames. He loved these things of impractical poetry.

We joined him in the afternoon, at a bar with its unchanging set of older clientele, where he laid out his finds for us on a sticky table. The bar was Ravi's pick: he liked places with regulars and an aesthetic of decrepitude. Once he pointed them out, we would quickly adjust to their charm, though they would have been invisible to us before, or felt uninviting.

There was nothing to drink but house wine served in scratched jugs. One glass in, Ravi would go around asking for a cigarette, a coin in hand. The regulars told him they weren't in the habit of selling their cigarettes but that he could have one as a fraternal offering.

Ravi quit smoking on Sunday nights and was back to hunting around for cigarettes on Wednesdays. When we teased him about the fact that he'd vowed not to smoke again, Ravi told us that he'd never said anything of the sort. If he wanted to, he said coyly, he could stop at the drop of a hat, but he didn't wish to deprive himself of the indulgence.

Manu and I didn't insist. We could relate to the pleasure of living a practice round before we set down the rules for good. Still, we were determined to find an apartment to buy.

Intimacy

Lena asked me if I would meet her after a doctor's appointment. She had discovered a bump above her gum while brushing her teeth. For a few days she ran her tongue and finger over the spot, hoping it would go away, before inally deciding to go to the dentist. It was a benign tumor and she would need to have a simple operation, but she worried she might not be able to go home alone afterward.

Just in case I'm groggy, she said. I know this is a hassle.

Of course, I told her. You can't go home alone.

I had never met Lena's friends, though I listened attentively whenever she mentioned them, trying to gauge where our friendship fit in her life of a native. In the beginning, I felt grateful to Lena for having made a space for me, when she already had a fully made life of her own. At the same time, I sometimes had the sense that I was Lena's only close friend, that she had no other obligations or bonds in her daily life. But how could that be when we had known each other for such a short time? I hadn't lived in my hometown for many years, and still, each trip back required me to conceal my visit from the various friends I wouldn't get a chance to see. Perhaps Lena gave off the impression of full intimacy to everyone she spent time with.

In any case, I was surprised that she'd asked me to accompany her. On the day of the operation, I bought a sandwich, a bottle of juice, and a pastry, which I put in a bag with a bar of nice-smelling soap. Lena had given me strict instructions to arrive at the very end, just in time to pick her up. And once she had been discharged, she kept repeating that she did not really need to be accompanied, after all, and that I should just go home and she would take the metro back. I had already called us a cab.

I'm totally fine, she said. But I could tell that she was rattled. Her eyes looked large and mute behind the bandage.

When we arrived at her building, she didn't invite me upstairs. She didn't take the bag of snacks, either.

Take them to Manu, she said.

I wanted to tell her it was all right, it even made me happy. I wished she would ask me for things more often. This was what I had in mind when I imagined growing native to a place—this sense that I was needed in someone else's life.

Thank you for coming, Lena said. I'm sorry that I wasted your day.

Division of Labor

My grandmother had begun to lose control over her bladder and rushed to the toilet at night, pee trailing behind her. My mother recounted with frustration how she woke up daily to the stains in the hallway, which she wiped with soap before getting ready for work. My grandmother was too stubborn to use diapers; she was neither bedridden nor senile, she insisted, even if it meant that my mother would have to clean up after her every morning. She must have been waiting for things to go back to the way they were, not willing to acknowledge that there is no going back from old age.

I was upset on my mother's behalf and sad on my grandmother's. I didn't ask her why she wasn't wearing her diapers. Instead, I asked her to tell me about when she was young.

I was the most beautiful of the group, my grandmother began. My waist measured fifty-three centimeters.

It had been many months since I'd last visited my grandmother, when Manu and I went for a week, but I hadn't really spent time with her then. She was left out of conversations with Manu because it was tiring to translate everything. She was relegated to the head of the table and kept quiet while the rest of us talked. She was too proud to butt in and waited indignantly to be included. It was a relief to be back in the city and talk to her on the phone.

I called her on Thursday mornings when I spent the day at home editing technical films. The money was too little to be substantial, which is why we spent it on dinners out on weekdays—our idea of an indulgence. Other things we considered indulgent were eating pastries for breakfast, going to the cinema on Sunday afternoons, watching two episodes of a detective show in a row. Sometimes, at the end of a day of editing, I would buy myself striped socks or sparkling tights.

I set up the editing work on the dining table and checked the time to make sure that my mother had left for work. I propped the telephone screen in front of my laptop. My grandmother recounted the developments in her television series and in the lives of distant relatives, barely distinguishing the real and imaginary plotlines. And she told me, from the beginning, the achievements of her youth. From time to time, she asked if I was listening, and when I nodded, she said:

Then look at me when I'm speaking to you.

In the Park

I come here on my lunch breaks and sit by the lake. I eat a sandwich from the bakery, then I walk around the park for some exercise. Otherwise, I sit at my desk all day long. I have so many problems from sitting.

Everything hurts. When I come to the park, I feel like I'm loosening up a little. Like the trees in the wind. It feels different here. But then I go back to my desk and it's all stiff again.

Principles of Kinship

It had been three months since we started our apartment hunt. I wondered whether we should look farther away from the city, explore the small towns we'd never been to. I'd finally told Lena about our search and asked whether she could think of any suburbs we might not know about.

Come this weekend to my mother's, Lena said.

It was a bizarre sort of invitation but I'd begun to learn that Lena was strange about things that mattered to her. The wrong line of questioning would make her retract.

We boarded a train from the central station and after an hour arrived in a small town. I had always assumed Lena had grown up in the city center, though I realized she'd never told me this outright. It was the way she carried herself, her air of the native.

The main street was a disorder of supermarkets and fast-food joints, teenagers hanging out on the sidewalk. Lena had been on edge during the ride. She talked distractedly, jumping from topic to topic, not really listening to my responses. Now, she hurried down the street and I rushed to keep up with her.

It dawned on me that in all the time I had known her, I had misread Lena's attempt to communicate the suffocation she felt in the city. She'd told me many times that she wanted to get away, and I'd interpreted her words as arrogance: that she'd had enough of the city's charms and riches, had grown bored. Whereas she had been saying the opposite. It wasn't her own arrogance but the city's that wore her down.

Lena's mother greeted us at the door and hugged us both. It had been so long since I had visited such a home and I realized that I hadn't brought anything as a gift. I mumbled something in apology and Lena's mother made a gesture as if swatting my words.

On the dining table was a heaping dish of fried peppers, another of herbed and spiced yogurt. A casserole of whole chicken.

You've really gone overboard, Lena said, but I could see that she was pleased rather than embarrassed.

Lena's mother was small and round. Her cheeks were stretched cheerfully, full of color, whereas Lena's were bony, what I thought of as a distinguishing character of city people, their gauntness like a mark of self-discipline. It now seemed that the look of the native was one Lena had adopted. In her mother's house, I could see another life for her.

What a feast, I said.

Hop on the train and come anytime, Lena's mother said. Tomorrow afternoon, I'm making lamb for everyone.

Everyone, Lena explained, is my brothers.

You should come for once, her mother said.

I'm working.

I don't know what sort of work this is, starving yourself, serving strangers.

She refilled our plates, despite our objections.

When we were leaving, she repeated that I should come back whenever I wanted.

My daughter's friends are my daughters, she said, and I was flooded with emotion. It was a life we'd given up long ago, Manu and I, by choice or circumstance, I wasn't quite sure. A life where we would have been sons and daughters to many people, could show up to eat unannounced.

On the walk back to the station, Lena asked me if I still wanted to live outside the city.

You're probably not used to the boonies, she said sarcastically.

Not at all, I told her. That was really nice.

Forms of Enchantment

By our bedside was a blue-green bowl filled with bundles of herbs and branches, tied together tightly like brooms.

Next to the bowl was a candlestick, a small lacquered box we'd found at the flea market, a lamp in the shape of a tulip. I never got tired of this assembly, those small and beautiful things gathered with mystery. Perhaps it was because these objects didn't quite belong to us—they were not part of an aesthetic either of us had grown up with.

At university, Manu and I had known people who burned sage, whose rooms were filled with objects of ritual from foreign countries. These people also had a knack for picking out clothes from yard sales and vintage shops—things that would have looked awkward on us, because we didn't have the right attitude, that sense of playful entitlement that was its own language.

Every time we burned herbs before going to bed, Manu would make a joke to ward off the feeling that we were impostors.

Shall we burn some trees?

Let's start a forest fire, I replied.

This was the great relief: that we did not consider each other strange.

Ancestors

On a Sunday afternoon, we went to the anthropology museum on the other side of town. The museum was dark and vast. The display cases were stacked full of masks, totems, and skulls.

We saw a collection of monolithic sculptures of shamans holding children with animal limbs. The shamans' faces looked unlike the faces we were accustomed to; I couldn't match their expressions to anything from my own life.

Manu was fascinated by the reconstruction of a sacrificial pool in which were placed shells, figurines, and a marble statue of a deity. The outer edges of the pool were lined with stones of hypnotic colors, velvety black and pale green, speckled red or struck with a bolt of ocher. Of course, we reminded each other, these beautiful objects were buried underground because their invisible value was deemed greater than their beauty.

Afterward, we decided to walk all the way back to our neighborhood. Winter was closing in, becoming darker. Every weekend we had an urge to make the most of the light. Midway home, we decided to sit down for a snack, having remembered that we had many vegetables in the fridge going bad.

We ordered beers and a plate of calamari.

I can't remember the last time I ate calamari, Manu said. I used to think it required a special occasion.

We can do whatever we like, I said.

We're adults, goddammit, Manu said, which was one of our sayings.

Goddammit, I snapped.

Goddammit. Manu smacked his hand on the table.

I asked what he'd liked most at the museum.

The oval stones for offering, he told me right away, and that made me feel sorry for the two of us, who had such little ceremony in our lives.

On our walk home, I picked up a stone and slipped it in my pocket.

Table Manners

Manu's parents came to visit. They stayed with us, even though the spare room had only a single bed. Manu and I gave them our room, and slept squeezed on the guest bed.

On the first morning of the visit, I woke up early and went to the bakery. Manu was going to make sausages. We set the table with candles to make things festive. We put out cloth napkins we'd bought before their arrival.

Manu's parents thought of our lives as a series of obstacles and were always worried about us. I wanted them to see that we had a good life, and that we enjoyed it. But despite my resolution, I was tired after a few hours. Manu's mother had put away the napkins before we even sat down, saying that it was a waste to soil them over a single breakfast. As we were clearing the table, she said she'd cook us dinner, so that we could have at least one proper meal.

As opposed to the trash we otherwise eat? Manu said. I said nothing.

Mama is just being caring, Manu's father said.

The parents presented a unified front to the external world, even when they were in disagreement. But when Manu's mother went to our bedroom to get dressed, his father came up to me and said breakfast had been excellent, trying to see if I was offended.

We took them to the river promenade and to a municipal museum that was free of charge. Manu's parents were worried about the costs of things. The goal was to spend time with them without spending money, so they could enjoy themselves unrestrained. Whereas my father would have made a show of it, as if he'd otherwise seem lacking as a parent. With him, our worry was that he would spend beyond his means. We adjusted to each visit, its particular needs, trying to make our parents believe that we were really not so different from them.

Manu's father was supposed to retire the following year, and he sat with Manu every evening at the dining table, going over accounts. Manu's mother and I looked through a home decoration magazine, pointing at the things we liked. Then we looked at photos of the grandchildren. Manu's mother turned to me.

And you? she asked. Soon?

I pretended not to understand what she was saying, even though I knew this many words of Manu's mother tongue. I got up and announced that I would make tea.

She turned to Manu and repeated the question. Manu mumbled something at her, then translated that we were still discussing the subject.

Right? he asked.

I nodded, though I was upset. I thought that he had an agenda; he wasn't really on my side. He was putting all the responsibility on me. I would probably bring it up at some point, the next time we had an argument. I was good at overlooking grievances for a bit, until I had enough stored up to pick a fight. Whenever we fought, entire lists would spill out of me, to Manu's surprise. I insisted that things never changed, counting the many instances when Manu had upset me in the same way, and Manu replied that I was rounding things up too drastically, arriving at unreal conclusions.

But soon after, he would remind me that we were the *T*s, that it wasn't worth it. I would pause and, having no counterargument, give him a reluctant hug, which quickly softened its way to a real one.

On Manu's parents' last evening, we bought meats and cheeses and sat around the table recounting the trip. When it was time for bed, Manu's mother began to cry. We all tried our hand at consoling her, but she waved us away. Once we retreated, however, she called after us that we could never understand a mother's feelings.

The day of their departure, after we'd seen them off, we mopped and vacuumed the floors, changed sheets, and moved our things back to the bedroom. Manu opened a bottle of wine in the afternoon, to signal that life was restored to its previous state. But I'd grown accustomed to him behaving as a son, and couldn't immediately readjust my sight.

Fear of the Old

A few days later, we met up with Ravi at our bar. Beers, a basket of fries. We told him about all the tense and funny moments of the parents' visit.

It's tough to see parents age, Ravi said. Mine get a little stranger every year.

Manu argued that his parents still had it together. Parents are bound to be a little strange, he said. They're parents.

At some point, Ravi said, you're the one humoring them. That's when you know you're already old and your parents are older.

It occurred to me that we didn't know anything about Ravi's family. He, too, had never introduced them to us. Perhaps he felt the same apprehension as I did, that his parents would dismiss our friendship. Or maybe he dreaded consolidating his different selves.

I asked what he did with his parents on their visits.

All the same parent stuff, Ravi said.

Which is what?

We go places, we eat, we get annoyed at one another. We try to deal with unsolicited advice.

I'd like to meet them next time, I said.

Sure, Ravi said, which meant it was unlikely.

I mean it, I told him, it's crazy we haven't met one another's families.

Manu suggested getting another round of beers.

I reminded him that he had to go to work the next day.

It's his work, Ravi said. Let's not micromanage.

Unless *you* don't feel like another round, Manu said.

No, I said, it's fine. I was contemplating a more adult life. Still, it made me happy that Ravi and Manu remained true to our group.

Close and Far Away

On the phone I told my mother about Manu's parents' visit. I made them sound comical—constantly imagining possible disasters—and my mother laughed and laughed. I wasn't being mean, only trying to be affectionate toward my mother. It was a statement of loyalty with a roundabout emotional logic: a way of saying that I wasn't part of any other family.

I told her with relish about Manu's mother's proposal to cook for us, and how she'd put away the cloth napkins. We laughed again, though this time I felt I'd gone too far.

Our families had met twice before, once at our wedding and once before when we decided to get married. Manu's mother had cried on both occasions. I was used to it by then; I could interpret the emotions that overcame her, the mix of worry and love. But my mother had been perplexed. Perhaps even more so because she, too, understood the cause for tears—that we would most certainly live far from our families for the rest of our lives. Perhaps she had first taken arms against my mother-in-law for expressing the sorrow so openly.

And now it's time for your visit, I told my mother.

Let's give Manu some time to breathe, my mother said. She sometimes talked about Manu as if he were half-child, half-old man, whose limits needed to be respected. This version of him was evoked during my family's visits, as well as during the few arguments I recounted—none of them serious, which was why I told her about them.

Asya, my mother said. Sweetheart, don't try his patience.

I played along with her vision of a marriage where the couple was entangled in a rigid and elaborate dance, whose harmony would be disrupted by stepping out of line. I didn't say that I considered it a ludicrous vision of love; that Manu and I were not at the mercy of simple manners.

In the Park

I started coming here when I moved to the city for university. No one in our group had very much money— none of us were from the city. There used to be a bar next to the park where we went after class. The owner poured us pints at half price and we carried some kegs for him. On weekends we came to the park to play cards. I think students these days do so many other things. They don't just sit in parks goofing about. But it was a good time. We sat behind the gazebo by the bushes, away from the guards. You know, we would smoke or whatever. I haven't seen most of those guys in a few years. We all got jobs, some of them left the city. Sometimes I also think about going back home. My family is all there. But that's just how it is; once you move it's easy to stay.

Future Selves

We viewed another house in the suburbs, at the end of the northern line. Outside the station, young boys stood smoking, huddled in groups. Others were selling loose cigarettes from plastic bags. I heard people speaking my mother tongue but I didn't feel comforted.

We were walking quickly, to get past the main street, which was too crowded. Then we turned a corner and the street was lined with trees and stone houses.

The owners—a couple our age—let us into the garden with a tunnel of blackberry bushes. They were both architects.

This house is our first child, the man told us, and the woman wrapped her hands around her rounded belly. They were moving away from the city, to a farmhouse they would renovate in time. I had somehow known they were going to say this—about the farmhouse, the renovation, leaving the city. I could practically list the reasons why: their child raised in nature, with space to play, among other children who were comfortable in the world, who could name trees and flowers and fruits. Then there was the pace of the city, the anonymity, the stress; there was the wish to live another type of life, with real neighbors and homegrown vegetables. I felt stifled by the clarity of my knowledge, which seemed unreal, or too real. As if everyone ended up living the same sort of life, describing it with the same words. With enough focus, I could probably predict our lives as well, the types of people we would resemble. There was something inevitable in choosing, in looking ahead: there were only so many options. But just now, I preferred not to think about it too much.

Inside, the woodstove was crackling. The wide-open living room and kitchen were streaked in shafts of light. On the dining table was a round, green-glazed teapot, and two small cups, communicating calm and pleasurable hours. I could never help wondering on our visits whether such things were left out on purpose.

The couple explained that they'd preserved as much of the original house as possible. The terra-cotta tiles, the stove, the wood frame. It was one of the many workers' houses of the past century, unique to this part of town, which had once been an industrial center and whose architecture was integral to the city's identity. All this, once again, had the ring of something I'd already heard, and I felt as if I could have given the tour of the house on their behalf. Whereas it didn't seem that the homes of those young men smoking around the station would also be cherished for their long-ago beauty in a hundred years. There would be no one, I thought, to praise their charm and dignity.

Manu was asking about the monthly cost of heating and the garbage collection. From his questions, I could tell he had already decided against the place. Why else would he be so specific in his inquiries? It was just a way to seem polite to the couple, to show interest in their first child. When we were leaving, Manu told them we would get in touch soon and I nodded my head.

We walked through another street, with a similar row of old houses. There were young couples, dogs of peculiar breeds, little shops that sold handmade things. Everything was so different from the crowds around the station, the men speaking my mother tongue just a few streets away. We found a neighborhood bar. Manu ordered a coffee. I ordered a vodka tonic.

You know what? Manu said. He asked for a vodka tonic as well.

What did you think? I asked.

It was nice, wasn't it?

Very nice.

Beautiful floors. And so much light.

I loved the blackberry tunnel.

We could have breakfasts outside.

All summer long.

Would you like that?

I think so.

We were letting some time pass before we could say outright that it wasn't for us. The simple recognition, quick and unmistakable, was always an occasion to celebrate, with the sense of freedom that overcame us, as if we'd escaped a terrible burden.

Vantage Point

I was now restless for change. When the cold weather set in, I made a soup of vegetables: parsnips, carrots, pumpkin.

And I baked a loaf of bread with chives and dill. I would tell my grandmother that I'd followed her advice to have herbs at home. It was one of the few things I could do: make her feel that her advice mattered in our lives.

My grandmother was fighting for her plot in the world. All her life, she'd tried marking this plot in various ways. At one time, she had been very beautiful—I believed this more from my grandmother's demeanor than from her pictures. To me, she looked the same as everyone else in black-and-white photos: eyebrows that were too thin, permed hair. But she had the manners of a woman who had been beautiful: there was vanity in her gestures, in her manicured hands making spirals as she spoke, in the way she dramatized her bitterness and joy. She had also been intelligent and talented, the recurring point in her stories about her high school years. She had played the lead role in a Molière play and was in the papers. The mayor had presented her with a bouquet of roses. Told like this, my grandmother sounded like a big deal. But then, I couldn't help putting the story in context. The mayor had probably done a favor to the school community by watching the play; a local paper had written a few paragraphs about the production, having nothing else to report. Still, this was the story that informed everything in my grandmother's life, her sense of perspective. I tried not to forget this when she started in on the details of the opening night. Instead, I told her that I wished I'd inherited a bit of her talent.

What a lot of nonsense, my grandmother responded. Of course you have all my talent.

Forms of Enchantment

On the first cold day, Lena and I went shopping together.

We met up in front of what looked like a butcher shop, with tall windows and linoleum floors. Instead of meat, there were piles of old sweaters, racks of coats and dresses, hats and bags hanging from hooks.

What're you looking for? I asked Lena. She shrugged, as if this were a meaningless question.

She walked through the stacks, piling clothes onto one arm. I had picked a few things as well, but I felt like an impostor in Lena's presence.

Here, she said, handing me a green velvet jacket. The silk lining peeking out of the folded cuffs was the color of saffron.

I stared at the strange and beautiful garment.

When would I ever wear that? I asked.

Lena looked a little bored with me.

You can wear it to your gala, she said.

From her point of view, I realized, the activity was neither frivolous nor practical, but an exercise in imagination.

I bought the jacket and Lena bought a pair of high-waisted linen trousers, the type one might wear on a safari. That is to say, the type that conjured a character. I was endlessly interested in Lena's personas, their multiplicity and flare. Sure enough, once we left the shop and sat down, Lena told me that these types of trousers were ones she associated with short-haired actresses who spoke with enigmatic charm.

Over tea, we talked about the women we had admired as children. Characters from movies or charismatic friends of our mothers', whose speech, gestures, and outfits we'd committed to memory. I marveled at Lena's methodical listing—she knew precisely what she had borrowed from each woman and was now assembling the individual parts in fresh combinations.

That evening, I had an idea to hang the jacket on the back of my chair, to remind me of something as I edited. I didn't know quite what I should remember, but I would recall that first sight of the jacket, its impractical glory.

Boundaries

Ravi, Manu, and I had a horror of therapy. We liked to say with self-congratulation that such things were unheard of in the places where we'd grown up—which wasn't even true. Still, we frowned on this way of life as unnecessarily elaborate, a vain pursuit of the self, which we somehow equated with capitalism. It seemed, we mused, that therapy increased consumption, not only because the foreigners spent small fortunes chatting away to their therapists every week, but also because these sessions unleashed a certain decadence in them, a drive to constantly treat themselves to things by virtue of the repeated affirmation that they were worthy, that they should abandon their guilt and fully enjoy their lives. Perhaps we were simplifying the experience, since none of us had ever spoken to a therapist. And we were proud of this fact to the point of obstinacy. Our disdain was a binding element of our friendship, a way to set ourselves apart. And once articulated, we stuck to it like a motto, an animating spirit of our group.

We sensed smugness in the foreigners' repeated disclaimer that they were doing work on themselves, as if the psyche were a house for remodeling, its parts identifiable as rooms and walls and beams, its leaks and fissures possible to fix. And it seemed there was always a limit to how genuinely we would be able to know them, because the constant calibration of their own well-being wouldn't allow true intimacy. *Stinginess* was the definition Manu, Ravi, and I finally settled on, one night when we were the last ones left at a bar.

For Manu, the stinginess resulted from too much time contemplating oneself. For Ravi, it came from a rigidity about one's personal upkeep. At gatherings with the foreigners, he went on, someone would always announce, too soon and without apology, that they should get going: they needed to wake up early and go for their morning run, they couldn't risk being groggy the next day. Ravi was convinced that this lack of generosity toward the collective camaraderie was also a result of therapy, which, he said, was the equivalent of an education in selfishness. It came from the relentless training they'd received in drawing boundaries, protecting themselves, constantly acknowledging their unique value: all this was the product of a maniacal individualism. I joked that Ravi simply didn't like to see people acting responsibly.

It's not that, Ravi said solemnly. I just don't like when people take themselves so seriously. We all have work to do the next day.

I was kidding, I said.

Also, Ravi went on, why is personal maintenance the only form of responsibility?

Showing up at work late and hungover hardly qualifies as being responsible, I offered.

The problem, Ravi said, was that the products of endless therapy—those sanitary people with their pristine boundaries and undisturbed routines—were increasingly becoming the norm.

But just imagine our own parents, he said. Imagine our hometowns where everyone is in everyone's business. What would it be like for an auntie to say she's setting boundaries and please don't rely on her for family meals from now on?

The auntie uprising! Manu said.

Good for her, I said. But I could see Ravi's point. And I secretly hoped those aunties would remain as they were, protecting an ancient order.

Hard Times

Manu was on the phone with his brother. He got up from the couch and went to the bedroom, closing the door behind him. He did this sometimes, stretching on the bed while he talked, and I would remind him afterward of a childhood rule about outside clothes and bedsheets. But this time, I could hear that he sounded troubled. There was a minute of near shouting, then a weary goodbye. A moment later, he came back to the living room.

My brother's enrolling the children in a religious school, he said.

Oh, I said, but I didn't quite understand.

These schools are awful, Manu said. They're like prisons. Or cults or something.

That's really bad news, I said.

And he told me just like that, as if it was no big deal.

Why does he want the children to go there?

He said these people had really helped them out recently. He said they were so kind.

Classic, I said. Classic cult behavior.

His brother kept repeating that it had been a very hard year for them. Manu hadn't realized until then just how difficult, and he felt embarrassed.

We could send them some money, I suggested. We could send them my father's New Year's present.

I guess so, Manu said. It felt so lonely talking to his brother, having no way of seeing things as he did, and no way of making his brother understand how strange he sounded.

It makes no sense, he said. He's my brother.

A few days later, he brought up the subject with his parents during their weekly talk, which lasted exactly forty-five minutes. Once again, I heard Manu's voice getting tense. When he came to the living room, he looked very tired.

They're completely oblivious, he said. They said it would be good for the children to have a community like that.

He pulled at his hair.

What the hell, he said. He was on the verge of tears. They'd never have sent us there when we were young.

Manu, I said. I'm so sorry.

That evening when we had changed for bed and were preparing to smoke a joint, he told me, I feel so sad.

I know, I told him, those poor children. We'll make sure they spend their holidays with us and smoke some pot.

It's not that, Manu said. I should have known what was going on. This is my family.

Principles of Kinship

Lena was over for dinner one evening. I was taking my time in the kitchen so she and Manu could have a chance to talk.

From time to time I invited Lena to dinner to try out a familial configuration, but it was never very successful. Still, I kept trying, because there were only so many people in our daily lives to make a family.

Manu found Lena too dramatic, and I think Lena thought Manu was a little dull. She'd never told me so, but she never seemed engaged with anything Manu had to say, not that he made a great effort. Whenever the three of us were together, it seemed that Lena was even more sarcastic—that the things she and I made fun of turned into bitter commentaries, even accusations. But I understood that Lena felt out of place in her life, which made me feel closer to her.

I brought out the food, a platter in each hand, and Lena said that I was the picture of a perfect housewife.

I laughed and Manu frowned.

So, Lena said, is it always like this with you guys?
Asya cooks and you entertain?

Of course, Manu said. And after dinner I put up my
feet while my wife cleans up.

Not a surprise, Lena said. My perfect bourgeois friends.

You two, I said. Serve yourselves before the food gets
cold.

When she left, Manu told me he found her insufferable.

I knew you'd say that, I told him.

I guess I'm just bourgeois and predictable, he said.

She's just a little vulnerable, I said.

Well, Manu said, aren't we all.

In the Park

I just finished my evening run, and from here I'm going
to walk home. I do five loops, varying my speed, five
times a week. I'm fifty-five years old and I run at the
same pace as I did when I was forty. I'm proud of that.
I've run races, too. I always run alone. I find other people
a distraction. This park is good because it has soft trails.
The joints are a runner's primary asset. If you damage
them, game over. You have to pay attention to protein as
well. My wife and I rarely eat the same thing because
I'm very careful about all this. You can't just leave these
things to fate.

The Drinking Spirit

Ravi was over for lunch on a Saturday. I'd insisted on it as a way of establishing some rules.

Guys, I told them, we're always getting drunk for no reason and spending too much money.

They looked a little surprised, but they agreed to spend the day at home. I cooked pasta and roasted a tray of vegetables, and we watched a movie about a young woman trying to figure out what to do with her life. The film was particularly good at portraying the heroine's quirks, her self-mumblings, her jokes with her best friend, the little dances she performed alone.

After the movie, we were hungry again and decided to heat up leftovers. So we didn't feel sluggish, we first went out for a walk, all the way to the highway. We climbed up the overpass and watched the traffic flowing beneath us. When we returned, Manu and Ravi mixed drinks and I fried eggs to add to the vegetables. We sat back down at the table.

In many ways, Manu said, the character in the film resembled the foreigners, with her tailored quirks that were nonetheless not too quirky.

I bet she'd leave a party early because of her morning run, Ravi said.

You're so bothered by the fact that people aren't alcoholics, I said. It was the same conversation we always had.

It's not the drinking, Ravi said. It's the drinking *spirit*.

Someone with a drinking spirit, he explained, was a person who, when offered another round, would not refuse by making a point of their individual needs. Regardless of whether or not they were drinking, they'd welcome the continuation of the evening. This was one of the most important characteristics, he concluded, in a decent person. It was the embodiment of generosity.

You can't be serious, I said.

After kindness, he added.

And curiosity, Manu said.

What about honesty? I asked.

Okay, and then the drinking spirit.

I got up to find a notebook and pen. I sat down at the table to make a list. Number five, according to Manu and Ravi, was a sense of humor. I wrote that down, but I didn't think it was very important. I told them so.

No worries, Ravi said. We never thought you were funny, anyway.

By ten, it seemed to me that we'd covered our grounds: honest, kind, and curious. Funny, patient, humble, generous. Creative. A lover of nature and beauty.

Let's go up to a hundred, Ravi said.

It was a tedious task, but because we'd set down the *spirit*, I couldn't object.

By the time we finished, the last metro had already stopped running. I'd considered telling Ravi that if he wanted to get home, he should probably leave. Ravi was focused on the list. Again, I reminded myself of the drinking spirit, even though I wanted to spend the following day calmly. I was on edge, thinking that we would prepare another big meal the following morning, feel restless and stale sitting around. Neither Manu nor Ravi seemed bothered by any of it.

We made Ravi's bed all together then sat down for a nightcap. By the time we fell asleep, it was almost morning.

Outer and Inner Orbits

The following weekend, Sara came to visit us. There was our life in the city and there were all our lives elsewhere, floating in and out of the present.

I picked her up at the train station late in the evening.

Sara and I were friends from school. Years before, I would refer to her as my best friend, even though I knew that Sara found the term immature and did not like to be possessive of people. This summed up some aspect of our friendship—my eagerness and Sara's nonchalance.

I used to have the impression that Sara regarded me as somehow quaint, having been with Manu since adolescence, living without conflict. Whereas she moved from one partner to the next. But in recent years, she'd begun showing an interest in my relationship with Manu, trying to understand its constitution. She asked me about our arguments, our compromises, the things we learned from each other. I'd never thought about it that way. Manu and I simply got along: we could sit together in silence; we didn't really work to maintain a state of harmony. I felt secure with him, like being indoors during a downpour. But I couldn't tell Sara that we'd simply been lucky. So that I wouldn't seem smug, I came up with reasons, pointed to our discipline in maintaining equilibrium, the natural cycles and difficulties that we weathered.

Sara's relationships resembled classes in self-improvement: one boyfriend was well-read in art history and literature, and gave Sara many books that had formed his imagination. Another traveled widely, to places outside of the touristic experience, unreachable by regular transport and untainted by outsiders, whose existence one doubted increasingly. Yet another knew the basics of survival. He lived on very little, spent months at a time in tents, up on mountains and in the woods. He had taken Sara with him, they had cooked on stones, gathered wood, swum in rivers. The relationships all ended in a similar fashion. There was the partners' unwillingness to change, as well as Sara's reluctance to express her desire that the men take part in her life just as she had taken part in theirs. But her entry into the relationships was always a rejection of her own ways—to know and to experience more of the other person—taking on shadow selves that she inhabited for stretches at a time.

At home, Manu and I set out bowls of nuts and fruits and lit candles. Sara had brought us a bottle of whiskey, the same one she always brought, which we usually finished by the end of her visits. We opened it right away.

I love being here, Sara said.

Take it all in, I told her. We're looking for another flat.

I won't allow it, Sara said.

I told her about the places we'd seen so far, and my suspicion that daily objects were purposefully left out to curate specific ideas of home.

No, no, no, Sara protested. You can't move. This is my childhood home.

The following morning when Sara woke up, Manu and I were already in the living room, drinking coffee. It pleased me that Sara felt comfortable enough to sleep in. Somehow this seemed like a sign that our lives were real.

What's on the menu? she asked, stretching dramatically at the doorway.

We walked all day, stopping for food and coffee, moving from one story to the next. Sara told us about a woman with whom she had become close, who seemed very charming to her at the beginning but whose vulnerabilities were increasingly rising to the surface as their friendship solidified. And about a man she'd been involved with for several months, whom she had believed at first to be a soulmate—so strong was their connection.

But she related the affair lightly, almost mockingly, as if to say that she saw right through her own infatuation.

I told her about my visit to Lena's mother's house, when I'd realized that my reading of Lena's character had been off this whole time. Sara was skeptical.

There's no single reading, she said. We're different people in different situations. This Lena just sounds like a city girl who grew up in the suburbs.

It was surprising to hear it summed up like this; I seemed to have a knack for complicating the point. But I wondered whether Sara was being defensive; stating her own right to shift guises with each relationship. Still, I didn't challenge her because we had so little time together. I would share my observations with Manu instead, when he and I sat down to unpack the weekend. It was always a delicious moment.

That evening we met up with Ravi at a restaurant we'd never been to, more stylish than the places we usually frequented. In this way, it seemed, even our closest friends would not get to see what our lives were like.

Over dinner, we told Sara about our list of one hundred attributes. Manu and Ravi took turns explaining the drinking spirit.

That's a value I stand by, Sara said, and suggested going to a bar afterward.

Trying to tick all the boxes, Ravi teased.

At the bar, he bought us drinks, wrestling Sara at the counter.

Oh come on, Sara said. Give me a chance to be a good guest.

Guests do as their hosts tell them, Ravi said.

We were all in great spirits, but I had the sense that Manu and I might be getting in the way.

We were too tired the following day to plan an outing. I worried that Sara might be disappointed about the previous evening. We'd all woken up with hangovers, and Sara had gone back to the bedroom after pouring herself a cup of coffee. Manu was also sullen, which upset me. I ran back and forth through a mental monologue: After so many years, surely Sara was a friend to both of us. It hurt me that he could be so moody. Just recently, I had put up with him and Ravi lazing through an entire weekend. How many times a year did we see Sara, to be grumpy on her second day? She'd come all this way to visit us. I thought bitterly that Sara was mistaken about me and Manu; our harmony was only an illusion.

Manu went out to get bread and I made pancakes. When he came back, Sara was in the shower.

What is it? I asked. Why are you so grumpy?

He protested that he wasn't.

She's our friend. She's only here for two days.

I know, Manu said. He held my face. I'm just a little sleepy.

I told him I was worried he wasn't having a good weekend and that he was upset with me for Sara's presence.

One more thing to worry about, Manu said, which was a joke we had, that I would always find something in the midst of our happiness.

The Living and the Dead

Were we happy, then?

I was always aware that sorrow might be around the corner. Manu didn't live in constant fear that something bad would happen to us. At times, I had an urge to alert him to all the possibilities I'd foreseen.

I could get sick. Manu could get sick. Our parents could get sick. In fact, it was certain that they would, sooner or later. There would be the moment when we'd receive a call about an accident, a diagnosis. With the news, we might lose our grounding. We would not know where to live, where to root our loyalties. We might grow resentful toward each other, or estranged.

And there were the bigger scenarios I played out. I had read about the depression caused by the decline of nature and, like hypochondriacal medical students imagining the symptoms they learned from textbooks, I sometimes convinced myself that I had already fallen prey to it. I thought ahead to the time—ten years on, twenty—when there would be fewer life-forms around. I imagined a barren, cracked, and withered landscape.

Though in reality, things would probably appear no different to me than they did now: it was likely not the spruce trees and chestnuts and decorative ginkgoes of the city that would die en masse, or the grass and tulips and hydrangeas. I would still be surrounded by dogs and cats, crows and pigeons, ants, flies, and spiders. I had seen so little of the nature whose extinction I feared, an insight that did nothing to soothe me.

I did not share these bigger worries. After all, panic assaulted us daily, in newspapers and documentaries, in graffiti and posters and demonstrations. Perhaps I was even afraid that Manu might disregard them, relieved that this was my worry, rather than something personal and intimate. Manu believed in the living, and he was glad for the beauty while it lasted.

In the Park

I used to consider the playgrounds a waste of park space. I would think, Why put up all these things when you can play around trees? Now I come to the playground every day with my daughter. In fact, I can no longer recall what the rest of the park looks like. To me, it's just this playground, beneath this great cypress. I'm grateful to whoever built it.

Music

Tereza called to ask whether we would like to come with her to a concert; she had extra tickets from a charity she had been a member of for years. The program was Brahms and Dvořák and Paganini, she said, none of which sounded very interesting to us. We told her we'd be happy to go.

A week before the concert, she arranged for the taxi. It would pick us up two and a half hours before the event.

Isn't that a bit early? I asked.

Better be safe, Tereza said.

When we got in the car, the smell of perfume was overwhelming. Tereza was dressed in a brocade jacket, with a flurry of scarves and pins and rings.

These are my dear friends, she told the taxi driver, then gave him meticulous directions to the concert hall even though the route was up on his screen.

The reception was teeming with old women. Except for the ushers, Manu and I were the only young faces around. Then we knew why we'd been brought along, and with so much time to spare. Tereza presented us one by one to her friends.

Manu winked at me.

Let's spoil her rotten, I whispered.

Manu flattered all the old women we were introduced to. He rested his hand on their arms, beaming his largest smile. The women were delighted. It was all for Tereza's sake.

By the time we took our seats, Tereza was flushed with excitement. She read the program out loud, exclaimed when the music started. A few people around us shushed her and Tereza shouted that she was very sorry. By Dvořák, she was asleep.

When the taxi brought us back home, we went upstairs with Tereza and waited until she found her keys and managed to fit them in the lock. Once she was inside, we thanked her for the invitation.

Bless you, Tereza told us. God bless you both.

Visions of the Future

We kept clicking through listings for apartments. They all seemed fine, which was depressing.

If we won the lottery, Manu asked, what would we buy?

I closed my eyes. First, I found myself standing on a balcony, looking out at the city rooftops. Next, I was on a hill, with the sea below. From my imaginary vista, I turned back to look inside. For a moment it appeared chic and sparse, then cluttered and homey.

I guess some place high up, I told Manu. With a nice view.

Okay, Manu said. We could manage that even without the lottery.

The green velvet jacket was still hanging behind my chair. I hadn't worn it yet, but I was encouraged by its reminder of how I wanted to be in the world. The definition changed every time I articulated it to myself but the feeling was palpable. Playful, assertive, and a bit old-fashioned.

So there was the green jacket, for a start.

And there was our breakfast ritual, before Manu went to work.

There were the stones our ancestors had placed at burial sites.

All these were elements with which I wanted to build a home.

And then I thought of the Great Dame, sitting on a café terrace. I couldn't tell immediately what about this image compelled me, but I decided to hold on to it.

Mythologies of the Future

I hadn't spoken to my father since his visit. We didn't know how to chat with each other, to talk about our days. Still, we believed that we were close; out of principle, I suppose, about what it meant to be a parent and child.

After a long time, I would call him or he would call me. It was worse when he called. It meant that I had let too much time pass. This time it was my father.

How are you?

Good, I said. I added that we had been very busy, as a way of explaining my silence.

And your health?

All good.

Make sure you're getting rest.

And you?

All the same.

There was also the sense that we were merely checking up on each other while I was away on a long trip, and that we would fill in the details once I returned.

My mother kept up with every small thing: a movie we'd seen, what type of flowers I'd bought for the week. She knew what time we ate, when we were likely to be home. She never asked why I was recounting her the details of my day, whereas I worried when talking to my father that everything I told him should have a point. But beneath both lay the same impossible hope, unstated, that one day soon I would return and until then we were whiling away the time.

In the Park

We come here with my friend to practice our songs. We write all the lyrics. We find the beats online. There are many ways to find an audience. If you're good enough, millions of people will listen to you. We practice every day to be good enough. Sometimes people stop and watch us. For a moment or a whole song. We just keep going. You begin to feel something building, between our songs and the people. That's because we're speaking for them, too.

Division of Labor

I met up with Ravi while Manu was at work. We were both a little sheepish about the fact that we were hanging out on a weekday afternoon, as if this was a sign of degeneracy, though Ravi acted more nonchalant about it. Still, we both thought of Manu as more adult than us, with his fixed routine and salary, his knowledge of public holidays and long weekends. It wasn't a work ethic that brought him to the office every morning, but simple obligation. Like parents, I thought, who didn't necessarily choose to feed and dress their children out of passion or interest, but simply because they had to. This was one reason why I found it difficult to imagine my life as a parent; I contemplated every action and routine, wondering whether it was the right one for me.

Ravi wasn't teaching that afternoon and I didn't really feel like filming. The previous day, I'd spent many hours at the park talking to people. In my last interview, a woman who had patiently answered all my questions added that she was there for a moment of calm and quiet. I came home feeling uneasy.

Ravi ordered a beer with his lunch, but I said I couldn't bring myself to be so indulgent.

It's totally arbitrary that you're feeling guilty, he said.

Not so arbitrary, I corrected. I mean, it is a weekday.

You work on your own time, Ravi said. You have to live without apology.

Was this something I wanted?

The green jacket, the burial stones, living without apology. I wasn't sure.

Ravi often brought up a childhood friend of his who, some years ago, had made a successful film. It was also a terrible film, according to Ravi, popular for a few months then quickly forgotten. And yet, the friend had made enough money and connections that he now lived traveling from country to country on a year-round holiday. He'd come to the city once or twice and invited Ravi along to expensive restaurants and to a nightclub. Ravi told us about all of it with a mix of distaste and awe. The friend didn't seem like a very interesting person, though there was nothing wrong with him, either. Manu and I could never figure out what it was that made him so alluring and so troubling to Ravi, who reported to us all the mundane details of the friend's life, the cities he'd been to, the people he hung out with. And he said about this friend that he was completely unapologetic about having a good time.

We were sitting outside, even though it was too cold. I'd come prepared, in a wool hat and parka, because I knew I'd join Ravi for a cigarette midmeal. Later, I might be apologetic toward Manu, when he smelled the smoke on my clothes. He didn't like it when I smoked even though he didn't mind smoking joints. He claimed there was some logic to it. And he didn't like when I apologized: it made no sense, he said, it wasn't about him. I agreed but I still felt apologetic.

I thought it was not so bad to live with some amount of apology. Without it, there would be nothing at all holding us in place.

Even so, I finally ordered a glass of wine. Great clouds had gathered above us and the wind was threatening to blow away the table mats. I pulled the sleeves of my sweater over my freezing fingers. By the time our orders arrived, our napkins were damp with the first drops of rain. The waitress asked if we would like to come inside and we told her that we were fine. Ravi took out two cigarettes and tried lighting mine with cupped hands. The cigarette was damp, too, and wouldn't light up. By now it was really raining so we put out the half-smoldering cigarettes and went inside with our plates. Our glasses were still out on the table, the contents thinning with rainwater. The waitress looked annoyed that she had to go out and collect them. We apologized to her.

The rain was pounding when we finished eating and we parted ways without smoking.

Privacy

On video one afternoon, my mother's signs of aging took me by surprise. She leaned into the screen so I mostly saw her neck, saggier than it would appear if she were sitting across from me. There were two deep ridges around her mouth. Because I felt sad, I scolded her.

Hold up your video properly, you're basically showing me the floor.

Let's see, my mother said, and leaned in closer, knotting her eyebrows. I felt angry that she wasn't self-conscious about the way she looked. She couldn't just let go of herself, I protested silently. She had to stand up to time.

It was one of the facts of my life that my mother was beautiful and young: like a birthmark, a distinguishing trait. I'd always taken my time because of it. When I was at university, my mother was still blooming into another

state of beauty, a real one, not just a second-place conso-
lation. My mother had never found herself beautiful,
which only heightened the fact.

Years ago, I had made a film about her: She is clearing
out the clothes in her wardrobe. They are protected with
long plastic casings. She takes out a wool dress, a taffeta
skirt and matching jacket, a tweed vest. She admires the
clothes, without sparing any admiration for herself.

Over video that afternoon, we were having tea and
cake. Walnut for my mother, lemon for me. We held up
our plates to the screen.

What a treat, my mother said. Even after all this time,
technological intimacy continued to thrill her. I told her
about Sara's visit.

Is she still single? my mother asked.

My grandmother's head appeared in the screen.

Who? she said.

No one you know, my mother said.

Who's single?

Just a friend of mine, Grandma.

I couldn't tell her to move out of the screen so that my
mother and I could talk in peace. My mother couldn't do
so either, out of manners rather than kindness. My grandmother cut herself a slice of cake and sat down. Once my
mother finished her cake, we decided to hang up.

What a big rush, my grandmother said.

I'll call you later, I said.

All right, my mother and grandmother said in chorus.

Ways to Live

At the beer bar, we overheard a conversation about an abbey outside the city that produced a world-famous beer. Part of its allure was that it could be tasted only at the local pub: the monks produced just enough to sustain themselves. They didn't believe in making a profit.

A few weekends later, we rented a car to go on a pilgrimage. Manu would drive. I told Ravi to take the front seat. We had several playlists prepared for the ride. It felt momentous, this new experience in our friendship, though we all acted nonchalant. Once we left the city, we joyfully rolled down the windows, even if it was bitingly cold.

On the way, Manu told us about a program he'd listened to, profiling a group of adults who housed imaginary voices, with whom they conversed daily from childhood onward. These people weren't mad, he clarified. They had regular jobs, partners, children. They were sensible enough to know that the voices would be viewed with worry by their friends and family. So they continued their imaginary relationships in secret.

But they had online forums, to allow the voices to talk to one another. They even traveled long distances for their imaginary friends to meet. The radio program focused on one woman whose husband had filed for a divorce upon discovering about his wife's secondary life. There'd been no infidelity as such, but the husband expressed his sense of betrayal, the shock to learn that he had never really known his partner.

What an idiot, Ravi declared. He was adamant that there should be mystery in a relationship. It was boring to want to know the entirety of a person. Besides, it was impossible.

Manu and I tended to agree with him. Still, we could understand how lonely the husband must have felt.

What if, Manu asked, I discovered that Asya has been sneaking off to a knitting club every week? I might feel abandoned.

Couldn't you give me a more alluring double life? I pleaded.

We arrived at the abbey at sunset. We dropped off our bags at the cottage we had rented for the night and walked the suburban road to the abbey and adjacent pub. When we entered, the locals lifted their heads to take in the foreigners in their midst. There was only the one beer on offer, as well as a selection of simple, hearty foods. We ordered at the bar but, feeling too conspicuous, moved to a back table.

The beer was dark and strong and creamy. It was, we all agreed, the best we'd ever had.

After the long drive and a pint, we were all tipsy. Manu suggested getting a crate to bring to the cottage, but the beer wasn't for sale in bottles. If we wanted, the bartender told us, we could take our glasses with us and bring them back later. If the pub was closed, we could just leave them at the door.

That's the way to live, Ravi said. We were all touched by the spirit of the town, the devotion with which the beer was produced, the lack of vanity and greed.

We returned to the cottage with another round of pints. Ravi and Manu were excited at the prospect of a fire. They fiddled by the fireplace for a long time, loading and unloading logs, inserting twigs and pieces of newspaper. They seemed encouraged by the example of the monks; they wanted to devote themselves to the simple task and to execute it perfectly.

Meanwhile, I was feeling increasingly drunk. I walked past them to one of the bedrooms and lay down on the bed, waiting for the spinning to settle. It was nice, I thought, that I didn't feel awkward around Ravi. It felt good to be in the cottage altogether, with nowhere else to go. I was wondering if we were entering a new episode in our friendship when my eyes began to close and I gave myself up to sleep. By the time I came back to the living room, the fire was roaring. Ravi and Manu were passing a joint back and forth.

Where were you hiding? Ravi asked.

I told him I'd just returned from my secret knitting society.

Ah, Ravi said. Woman of mystery.

In the Park

My favorite tree is this very big one. Underneath, it's a different world. It feels like we're in someone's home. This is a copper beech. There are fifteen of them in the park. They are the most marvelous trees. In the fall, when all the others shed their leaves, they keep up for just a little longer.

Ceremonial Masks

Let's get dressed up one evening, Lena said.

And go where?

Lena gave me her look of total boredom, the one that made me feel lacking in imagination.

Somewhere dressy, she said. You should tell your boys.

This was how she referred to Manu and Ravi, and I could never tell whether there was a note of sarcasm in her tone. I hadn't told her that I found the term irritating and Lena had never told me outright that she would like to join the three of us on our activities.

That night, I told Manu about the plan.

Where will we go? he asked.

The point is to get dressed up.

The following weekend, we gathered at the metro for our journey to the posh neighborhoods, where we would go to a rooftop bar of Lena's choosing. Ravi was wearing a white shirt, as was Manu. I'd put on a cashmere cardigan I'd found crumpled at the back of the ward-robe, along with a few other nice clothes I never used, out of fear that they would get old.

We met Lena on the platform. Her hair was pinned up with a fuchsia flower. Long earrings shimmied by her cheekbones. She'd painted her eyes like a cat's.

Look at you, I said.

Good to see you, Ravi said formally. They had met only once before. During the metro ride, he told Lena about a movie that followed four farmers across a vast landscape. I knew that it had been months since he'd seen the film; we'd joked about how boring it was. Manu looked at me and twitched his eyebrows.

At the bar, we were told that we should have booked days in advance.

I can see an empty table, Lena insisted. We'll be done with our drinks by the time they arrive.

The maître d' asked us, politely, to leave.

This is unbelievable, Lena said. This fucking unbe-lievable place.

We took the elevator down with a stone-faced couple.

I can't believe it, Lena repeated, her eyes welling with tears. Clearly, the problem was greater than the table.

Look, Ravi told her, I actually think this is a stroke of luck.

Out on the street, he assured Lena that we wouldn't have had a good time on the rooftop anyway.

That place was terrible, he said. He was happy to be back on his own turf. Soon enough, he'd found us a seedy bar in his own style.

All dressed up, the bartender said to Lena.

Actually, Ravi told him, we're celebrating their marriage. He pointed to me and Manu. It was love at first sight.

He and I were the witnesses, Lena added, threading her arm through Ravi's.

The bartender offered us each a glass of mint liqueur.

To the newlyweds, he said, I wish you patience and good luck.

Ways to Live

Tereza asked us up for dinner and we said we would bring something to eat. It had been like this, ever since the time Tereza burned a pot of rice to charcoal: she'd gone to the bedroom to look through some old newspapers for a reason she couldn't remember when we arrived at the site of the burnt pot. We brought over a couple of dishes, Tereza set the table and put out a stack of books for us to read from as we ate.

This was another routine that we'd settled on, after an evening when Tereza asked us whether we knew any poems by heart. We fumbled around, one line here, one line there, but couldn't recall anything from start to finish.

Oh you must learn them, Tereza said. Later, they're great company.

She recited a few couplets in rhyme, and it seemed miraculous to us, the sudden music at the dinner table. We told her to continue. We couldn't get enough of it. Next time we were up, we proposed reading poems out loud, from the books on her shelves.

Tereza's appetite kept shrinking, week after week, and she only remembered to drink her wine when we toasted. But she could sit for a long time listening to us read. We read poets we'd never heard of, and others we had heard of too much to bother reading them.

In Tereza's presence, the world seemed less urgent. The poems cleared out spaces in us and filled us with their shapes. Sitting around the table, I felt that we should try and live like this, reassembling the world in poetry, where things were a little lopsided.

Now there was the green jacket, the ceremonial stones, breakfast with Manu, the Dame on the terrace, and the shapes of poems.

Altered States

The album cover was a photograph of the blind musician, his eyes closed, his beard long and sparkling like the Milky Way. We had bought the album when we were at university, on one of the weekends when we went to town, imagining ourselves in different futures. It was during these outings that we worked out what we liked and disliked, started inventing our mumbling speech, and called ourselves the Ts. We were trying out a joyful life.

The music of the blind man was like elves dancing in caves, or sea creatures moving their tentacles. It was like the universe, and like the forest undergrowth. All these things we had articulated when we ate something or other to expand our minds for a few hours. We would go somewhere very quiet, we would put out crayons and paper, and we would listen to the blind man as soon as our minds began to tilt. Sometimes we cried, sometimes we laughed. Sometimes we looked very intently at the world around us.

We still listened to the blind man in the city, though we no longer ate these things that tilted and stretched our minds. Even so, whenever the blind man's music started, we remembered the forest undergrowth—that other frequency that was a bit slower, a bit stranger, which made colors very bright and tender.

The Naïve Artists

There was an exhibition of naïve painters at the glass-domed gallery, whose shows were always an event. Posters hung all around the city and traveled on buses. They showed a field dotted with flowers. Their message was one of uncomplicated joy. I liked this easy attitude. I wanted to share it. Every time a bus passed me by, with the confetti of flowers, I wondered what more the naïve painters might be able to tell me.

Manu wasn't interested in the exhibition, because he thought those types of paintings would annoy him.

What types? I asked.

You know, he said, sort of silly.

I went with Lena instead. On the way, she told me that she and Ravi had been in touch after that evening, when she had pinned a flower to her hair.

We're going to meet up for a drink soon, she said. I felt hurt that Ravi hadn't told us about this.

Great, I said. Who wrote to whom?

Oh, I can't remember, Lena said, which made things clear.

He's sweet, she went on. But he seems a little lost. What does he do, anyway? He wouldn't give me a straight answer.

Lots of things, I said, feeling irritable. He goes on walks and he reads books and he watches movies.

You know what I mean, Lena said.

The naïve painters had all lived in the city in the past century. Some of the works were touching in their simplicity and provided more of the feeling I'd glimpsed from the posters on the city buses; others, with their bright colors, lacking technique and perspective, looked like unsuccessful attempts to scratch an itch. We stood in front of the flat, enormous head of a woman with pink skin and a field of daisies behind her.

It bothers me that these paintings were made in the first place, Lena said. They just take up space in the world.

I'm sure they were trying their best, I said.

They should've tried harder.

She was irritable, too.

After we left the museum, we walked down a shopping street in search of a restaurant. Every place we passed was too crowded, too expensive, or too dull. We finally decided to part ways. I didn't ask anything more about Ravi, and Lena didn't offer to tell me.

I was in a funny sort of mood; I couldn't name it. I got off the metro one stop early and went to a café. I ordered a glass of wine, which arrived with a bowl of peanuts. Once I'd finished both, I went out and asked a man for a cigarette. I held out a coin to him, as I'd seen Ravi do. The man didn't accept the coin but he wanted to chat for a bit, which I wearily obliged.

When I came home, I picked a fight with Manu. As I was taking off my coat, he said that he had made me a salad.

You shouldn't have made me anything, I said. You knew I'd be out with Lena.

You didn't say you were going to eat.

It's the first time in ages I've been out without you, I told him. You don't need to make a big deal.

Why would I make a big deal?

Just because you don't make an effort to meet anyone doesn't mean I have to do the same.

That's mean.

We're already so isolated as it is.

What about Ravi?

I mean seeing new people, and being out, and having new conversations.

We do all those things.

Getting drunk with Ravi is your idea of a fulfilling life.

Don't say that, Manu said.

I went to the room and got into bed. I heard Manu soon after, though I kept my eyes closed. He took off his clothes and came in to bed. He put his hand on my shoulder.

I'm sorry you're upset, he said, even though he knew I hated this particular remark. It was the type of thing the foreigners had learned to say from their hours of therapy, acknowledging the other person without really bringing themselves any closer. It was the surest way to make one lonely.

After a moment he added, I'm sorry I upset you.

I was too embarrassed to tell him anything so I tugged at his arm and held his hand.

In the Park

We come here every Tuesday and Thursday morning for our stretches. One of us takes the lead, the others follow. Look, you may think we're just a bunch of old women, but I can still touch my toes! We have a good time all together. The lesson is to live. That's why I love the park. The little paths and the lake. I love looking at everyone who comes here to sit and walk and stretch out on the grass. We're very strict about our park meetings. Because you have to take these things seriously. On Mondays and Wednesdays, we meet for tea. And a bit of cake, of course!

Forecast

By winter, our search for an apartment had disintegrated. We were drinking too much and eating too much, sleeping in on the weekends. We couldn't be bothered to do anything that was not on a direct metro line. We'd begun to think lazily that there was in fact no reason for us to take a loan. Why did we want to spend months settling into a new place, a new neighborhood? Why would we take on the worry of paying a mortgage. The enthusiasm with which we'd gone from place to place in autumn appeared to us now like a seasonal folly.

When my mother asked about our search, I told her we'd decided it wasn't so urgent.

Not just yet, she said, not until you have a child.

Out of the blue, my mother had tipped to intrusion. Some years ago, I'd heard her say to a relative that she didn't dare broach the subject with me. Another time, when my grandmother asked when I was planning on *getting to work*, my mother had stepped in to say that there was no need for harassment; we would decide when the time was right. Now she'd let go of all that. Weekly, she reminded me, even more brazenly than my grandmother, that there was absolutely no more time to waste. All these years, it became clear, she'd been humoring me; finally she was speaking her mind.

I rushed the conversation to its end.

I don't understand why you're upset, my mother said, and I replied with sadistic pleasure that she was acting just like my grandmother.

Well, my mother said, she and I agree about some obvious things.

I didn't tell Manu about the conversation, fearing he would side with my mother, but I did go back to the real estate website we'd checked several times a day all through autumn, clicking again and again on the same places we had already ruled out.

There were many new listings: one was in an alleyway we walked past often. We would make a detour to walk its length and pick houses. Manu liked the brick one, and I liked the white one, with ivy and sage in the windowsills. We argued about the superiority of our choices.

How can you possibly pick that, I would say. You're making a terrible mistake. Manu shrugged and told me that I could visit him from time to time if I wished.

The apartment for sale was in a building we had never noticed. A woman, a few years older than us, opened the door before we had even knocked. She asked us if we would like a glass of water, then walked us through the rooms. Everything about the place made sense to me: the jars of herbs above the oven, a basket filled with scarves. The woman worked from the upstairs room, her desk overlooking the leafy alleyway. Her pens and pencils were stacked satisfyingly in pottery.

And yet, something was wrong. Some misconfiguration, as if the rooms had been joined the wrong way. I dismissed the feeling and asked the woman whether she liked working from the upstairs room.

I love it, she said.

Are you moving away from the city? Manu asked.

No, the woman said. Just another neighborhood.

She didn't offer details, and we didn't know how to ask.

The price, I commented, was very reasonable given the location. I took Manu's hand. I said that we had always dreamed of living on this alleyway.

The woman stole a glance at our hands.

We're trying to sell it quickly, she said.

You and your partner?

My ex-husband.

We unlocked our hands and thanked her for the visit. The woman didn't wait for us to disappear from sight before closing the door.

Outside, the sky was high and welcoming. Manu had felt the misconfiguration as well, the sense of the walls pressing down. I said there was no real reason for us to feel this way. After all, we agreed, it really was a perfect apartment. And we said there must be something wrong in the way we were approaching this whole process, finding fault in perfectly good places. Still, we walked cheerfully back home.

The Invisible World

My grandmother had a simple explanation for why we hadn't felt comfortable in the seemingly perfect apartment: the whole place, she said, must be teeming with *them*.

With whom, Grandma?

Don't say their names out loud.

You mean, ghosts?

Nothing to do with ghosts, my grandmother said. They're their own thing. Neither human nor spirit.

What are they?

How can you not know the simplest things? my grandmother asked. I wondered about this as well.

Anyway, she continued, best not to talk about them too much. Let them be and get on with your own life.

Nomenclature

Tereza occasionally forgot our names, or called us by others. But she recited along to the poems we read, racing ahead to rhymes, her small, dotted hands tapping on the table.

One evening, we went up with a bowl of potato salad and another of pickled fish. These were the foods we imagined belonging to Tereza's childhood, though that was only a guess. In any case, the dishes pleased us in their poetry, as well as their content. We were greeted at the door by a suspicious, stylish woman.

We're Tereza's neighbors, I explained. We planned to have dinner together.

How adorable, the woman said. I know it's time to make an arrangement. She can't be at the mercy of neighbors feeding her.

We didn't have a chance to explain that the food we'd brought up was as much symbolic as it was practical.

My mother can barely dress herself these days.

Tereza had arrived at the door as well. She had dressed herself just fine, I thought, in a pink summer dress and wool cardigan.

Your lovely neighbors are here, the daughter said. Did you know they were going to bring you dinner?

It's our private club, Tereza said. But you're welcome to join this time.

Mama, the woman said, don't be strange.

We sat around the kitchen table, without books. Tereza started telling the story about the university students holding hands against soldiers. She was even more animated than usual, with her daughter to witness the gathering.

The daughter looked at me and Manu. Most of this stuff is made up, she said.

We ate quickly and got up to leave. Besides, the daughter had said dessert was absolutely out of the question.

But chocolate is poetry! Tereza chirped.

You'll put yourself in a coma, the daughter said.

At the door, she invited us for dinner the following weekend. There would be artists and writers we might want to meet. By this point, she'd gotten a general sense of us, with a few questions meant to situate who belonged where. She didn't invite Tereza, who was waving us goodbye.

That would be nice, I mumbled.

We'll let you know, Manu said.

Close and Far Away

On Manu's birthday I woke up feeling sad that I was all he had for a celebration. On those days, the haphazardness of our lives felt more pronounced. Or rather, I felt it might appear that way from the vantage point of our families, who woke up on our birthdays and imagined us all alone in the city.

I squeezed oranges, arranged toast and pastries and coffee on a tray. I put a flower on the tray as well, then changed my mind and put it back in its vase. It looked too much like something out of a magazine. Manu was up already but humoring my wish to bring him breakfast in bed, though neither of us had such a habit. He would probably have preferred coming to the bakery with me, drinking coffee at the dining table, and browsing the internet. But I wanted to distinguish the day.

I'd packed little things to fill a basket: books, chocolates, a striped scarf. There were stones and acorns I'd collected at the park, as well as a nice pen. Every year, I faced the problem that Manu had very few material desires; he would rather not have anything than too many things to choose from. He wore shorts with holes on the back pockets, white shirts turned gray with washing.

He surveyed the basket I'd brought to the bedside.

Look how nicely you wrapped everything, he said. Most of all, he loved the acorns.

His parents called. From the way Manu talked, sweet and solemn, I guessed his mother must be crying. My mother called, and my father. Manu's brother, who passed the phone one by one to the children. Then a cousin.

Thank you so much, Manu said over and over again. We wish you were here as well.

I was worried that the day would slip away on the phone, which it eventually did.

The next day was more cheerful, without the worry that we were making our families sad on happy days.

We went to celebrate at a restaurant down the street. We arrived with our books, had drinks under the heaters outside.

I'm having the best day, Manu said.

Over dinner, he posed to me his most hypothetical questions: What sort of farmers would we be? Which historical period? Astronaut or deep-sea diver? The questions made me feel that I couldn't survive a day in the world. I wouldn't be able to grow anything to eat, couldn't live through a war or plague, would get too sick on a rocket or submarine. I told him so.

I'll help you out, Manu said. We'll be fine.

We walked home tipsy, talking in our own language.

Let's get belligerent, Manu said.

Let's get belligerent and make a scene, I replied.

Afterlife

Tereza's daughter called me in panic.

She went for a walk and she hasn't come back. Do you know where she is?

I didn't.

I can't believe this, the daughter said. She's practically senile.

That's not true, I said. We'd seen Tereza a few nights ago, and she was in a great mood. We'd read sonnets for an hour straight. But I knew I wasn't being very helpful.

Listen, the daughter said. Do you think you could just walk down the street and take a look?

I was on my way out to meet Ravi and Manu at the beer bar. And I was annoyed at the daughter for the way she spoke about Tereza. Still, I wasn't the one who had to worry about my mother coming home after every walk. Not yet, anyway.

My phone rang again, just as I'd turned the corner.

She's back, the daughter said. She went to a museum then treated herself to a meal.

That's lovely, I said stubbornly. She should do that sort of thing more often.

Water from the Source

Then my mother called, one morning during the week. She never called in the mornings.

Sweetheart, she said very sweetly. I want to talk to you about something.

What happened?

Don't worry, but it's a bit troubling.

I held my breath.

Grandma is feeling a little sick.

My mother hadn't referred to my grandmother as Grandma since they started living together. It was a note of affection that I'd almost forgotten about, a bond uniting the three of us.

She had a stomachache some weeks ago and we went to see a doctor when it didn't get better. They found a small tumor.

What's small?

We'll need an operation.

Who's we? I asked pointlessly. You mean Grandma needs an operation.

Yes, that's what I mean.

I'll book a flight.

Not yet, my mother said. We'll tell you when you should come.

I kept things to myself for a few hours. I washed a load of laundry and hung it very carefully, pulling at all the cuffs and seams. I cleaned out my backpack. Then I called my grandmother.

Grandma, I said, I heard you have indigestion.

I always had troubles down there.

Are you in pain?

You don't worry about it, my grandmother said with authority.

In the evening, I told Manu. We were sitting on the couch with our dinner bowls. Manu was about to press play on the computer. In the previous episode of our show, the detective had caught a whiff of the suspect but hadn't told his partner, which put her in great danger as she went off on her own, with no one to look out for her.

Oh no, Manu said. Oh no. He put down his bowl. Let's book our tickets.

I didn't tell anyone else. There was the problem of expressing my devastation. Grandparents were meant to be old; they were meant to get sick. This was among the sorrows of life for which outsiders were not expected to pause their routines, to inconvenience themselves.

There were tragedies of the highest order that upended ordinary life, the ones that ushered in deviations of kindness. Then there was life itself, at every turn a devastation, which nevertheless did nothing to stall its flow.

The following day, I packed my equipment early and went to the park.

I sat on a bench near the fountain, from whose mouth poured water from a thermal spring. People came with water bottles and jars. A woman got in line with a bucket. I asked what she did with the water.

I drink it, she said, a little mockingly.

Why don't you drink from the tap in your home?

This water doesn't contain chemicals.

Which chemicals?

Fluoride and everything else the government pumps into us.

Why do you think they do that?

Because we no longer know how to live naturally.

But someone's installed a fountain here. Isn't that a sign that we know at least a little?

Sure.

Do you think everything that's added to water is bad, simply because it's not the water's natural state?

I realized that I'd taken a wrong turn in my questioning. Rather than trying to understand the woman, I had set out to contradict her. She picked up her bucket from the ground.

I'm just here to get my water, she said. You should ask someone else.

She filled up, then walked away.

I asked a middle-aged man why he was filling bottles from the fountain. He shrugged.

Does it taste better? I probed.

Not really, he said.

Behind him was a woman around the same age as my grandmother. She lived in the neighborhood and came here every day. It was just an excuse to get out of the house, she told me.

I might have had a proper conversation with her if I'd stayed longer, but I was feeling restless, so I decided to go back home. As I took off on my bike, coursing downhill, I realized I'd done nothing with my day. At least I could prepare dinner before Manu came. I stopped by the food co-op, where I went whenever I was determined to prepare a meal with care. I bought a cabbage and parsnips. A type of grain I had never heard of. I stopped at a butcher, too, and bought marrow. I would make a broth, I thought ambitiously, though I had never made one before.

By the time I returned to the apartment I was exhausted, for no reason at all, but tired to my bones nonetheless. I had written to my mother that morning but hadn't heard back, except for a quick line that the surgery was scheduled.

I lay on the bed with my street clothes—the great taboo of my childhood—and, having already decided to abandon the marrow, watched episodes of a show about girls with a different outfit for every scene.

Principles of Kinship

There was nothing to do but wait. It would always be this way, waiting for news to reach us in our city that wasn't even ours.

In the meantime, Sharon and Paul were hosting a brunch. Ravi was invited as well but told us he had other plans.

What sort of plans? I wrote.

Seeing some friends, a few errands. On the topic of Lena, he'd told us only that they had texted a few times. I found his evasiveness insulting, as if we were mere acquaintances.

I told Manu we should go to the brunch.

I'm so lazy, Manu said. Can't we make an excuse?

They're not that bad, I said.

I don't even understand why they keep inviting me.

Because they like you.

They like *you*, so they're letting me tag along.

This was true. I had no difficulty playing along with Sharon and Paul's social exuberance. I even enjoyed it, though I was a bit embarrassed in front of Manu.

We were greeted at the door by their daughter, Izzy. She was wearing a cape made out of plastic bags. She ran toward us with her arms open.

Are you a dragon? Manu asked.

No! Izzy said, and started running around him in circles.

The Tasmanian Devil?

She started running faster, then crashed into him.

Oh, she adores you, Sharon said.

Paul was frying eggs in a linen apron. He waved at us from behind the counter and told us to serve ourselves.

The table was laid with cheese and fruits and pastries. We'd started filling our plates when Izzy came to stand in front of us.

No eating, she said.

What if I say the magic password? I asked, reaching for a slice of bread.

Izzy was silent for a moment, then began to cry: a wall of piercing sound.

Okay, I said in a hurry. I'll put it back.

Izzy, stop bossing people around, Sharon shouted.

By the time we started eating, Izzy had been charming and capricious with all the guests. Sharon and Paul seemed delighted by her confidence; then they told her it was time to stop. She was given a plate of sweets and an iPad, and she sat hypnotized until we left in the late afternoon. From time to time, one of the guests would make a comment about how sweet she looked, her short legs dangling from the couch, though it was never suggested that she should join us at the table.

I tried adding it to the list: the green jacket, breakfast with Manu, ritual stones, a child on the couch with an iPad. But it was impossible to observe other people's deepest joys from the outside. At surface level, the situation didn't seem very pleasing.

Once the food was cleared, we sat around the table drinking coffee, then wine. The conversation interested all of us: TV shows, new bars, annoying encounters with the city's bureaucracy. Still, I had the sense that I was wasting Manu's afternoon, even if he seemed to be having a good time.

The sun had set by the time we got on our bikes. We took the scenic route back, the wind biting our cheeks. It started to rain softly and the lights of lampposts blurred in front of us. We passed many neighborhoods, a tour of our various years in the city: the year we moved, the year we had no friends and went to every museum, the year we met Ravi and ate out with him almost daily.

That night, when we'd changed for bed and Manu sat on the floor rolling a joint, I could barely recall anything from the brunch.

Did you have a good day? I asked.

Great, he said. I loved our ride back.

It might go on my list—the scenic bike ride. But I didn't know whether it was sturdy enough to stand its ground, the two of us biking around a foreign city.

Courtship

Ravi couldn't make it to the flea market, either. This time he told us that he was going to meet up with Lena.

Manu and I walked the stalls aimlessly. We bought a vase, for the sake of buying something, even though neither of us was committed to it. Then we got a newspaper cone of fried dough from the food truck and sat on a bench to eat, dipping the balls of dough in sugar. Usually at that time, we would be with Ravi at the decrepit bar.

What do you think the two of them talk about? I asked Manu.

I think Lena talks and Ravi listens.

I can't see them clicking, can you?

I sort of can.

But you always say Lena's dramatic.

Yeah. She's also pretty.

I don't think Ravi's her type. She said so herself.

What did she say?

That Ravi seemed lost.

People are mysterious, Manu said, unwilling to go into further speculation. I knew it was pathetic to continue talking about them, but I still wished Manu would humor me.

At home, I placed the vase in various settings but everywhere I tried, it looked unnecessary, even ugly, so I put it away in a cupboard with other objects I had bought without dedication, because they had briefly offered an idea of something.

Future Selves

A woman opened the door for us with a baby in her arms.

We're just finishing lunch, she said. Feel free to look around.

The bedroom was spacious, with a giant closet that had mirrors for doors. The marble bathroom was sparkling, with light bulbs all around the mirror. There wasn't a nail on the wall in the baby's room except for another mirror.

One part of the living room was cordoned off. Inside was wide-open carpet and a basket of plush and plastic toys. The other side was taken up by a television set. The woman told us that the supermarket, post office, and daycare were all within walking distance. I was struck by these places of proximity, at once poetic and banal. The neighbors were all young families, the woman continued. There were plans to renovate the building entrance in the next year. As she spoke, it became clear that she considered the apartment a very desirable one. Another couple was coming to view the place in a few minutes, she said, by way of asking us to leave.

We didn't propose going to a café. We felt depleted by the practicality and ease of such a life, with so many sparkling mirrors and no place for ceremonial stones. We walked all the way back home, over an hour, crossing into the old city and out again, to shake off the visit. What was the lesson, then? And how were we meant to live?

Life and Death

My grandmother looked purplish-white and startled. She nodded her head slightly off-screen while I told her things she already knew: the surgery was over, now she had to focus on getting stronger. When her eyes began to droop, my mother moved the screen toward herself, where she was sitting on an armchair beside the bed.

Thank you for the chocolates, she said. I'd sent a large box to the hospital, though I could see for myself that no one was in any state to eat them.

In the Park

I started coming to the park a few months ago, when I became pregnant. I used to have an idea that these months would be dreamy. I imagined myself a part of nature, surrounded by trees and birds. In reality, the park is close to the dentist's office. Otherwise I never come to this part of town. No, it isn't dreamy like I imagined. It's a violent time. I've lost two teeth already. I see the dentist every other week. But I worry that by easing the pains of my mouth, my swelling gums, I'm harming the baby—with the X-rays and anesthetics and antibiotics and hours of lying still. The doctors say these are approved procedures, but what do they know, really?

Ways to Live

More and more, the thought came to me that I didn't know anything about anything. At the weekend market we bought things we didn't know how to prepare: a freshwater fish shaped like a heart, herbs with small berries at the tip, a root the color of irises. But it seemed important to get them, these foods that had come into season. Had they really come into season? Perhaps they'd simply caught our attention that day.

On the way home, Manu pushed away on his scooter, which he took out on weekends, stopping to wait up when he went too far, coming back to circle around me.

Why can't you just walk the two blocks?

He circled around me again.

You're making me dizzy, I told him.

I was feeling very practical, out of a bad mood. That morning, my mother had sent me a photograph of my grandmother, her hair wet, a towel on her shoulders, sitting up at her hospital bed. Underneath, she'd typed: *Grandma sheep, clean and combed.* It was meant to make me happy and I felt wretched. I hadn't shown the photograph to Manu, but bossed him around instead, snapping at him for taking the wrong shopping bag, asking if he intended to go out without a coat and get sick, rushing him along when he stopped to watch the lobsters moving sluggishly at the fishmonger's stall.

I felt we were wasting time, that we should just hurry up and get on with things, even if we had nothing much planned for the rest of the day.

Let's sit down for a coffee somewhere, Manu said.

The fish will go bad.

Just for half an hour.

Whatever you want, I said, and Manu pretended not to hear my tone.

We went to the café closest to home. It wasn't a very nice one. Three men were drinking beers around a bowl of pretzels, and an old couple sat silently side by side.

Look, that's me, Manu said, meaning the old man. He was wearing a stained shirt. His wife had a sweet and silly expression. They were both a bit chubby and they looked content.

This was a game we'd played from the very beginning, back when we used to leave campus to wander around town. We would spot ourselves in old couples, especially those that were a little clumsy. We considered that a slightly pathetic appearance was in part a sign of their cheer, a lack of vanity with which they'd weathered the years. Looking at the couple with their drooping outfits, I could see another way to live.

When the waiter came, I suggested having pastries alongside our coffees.

I like how you're thinking, Manu said.

And I said, We're adults goddammit.

Outsiders

My grandmother was back from the hospital.

Look at Grandma's fancy bed, my mother said, tilting the screen for me to see. The bed moved up and down with a remote control. My grandmother lay speechless and pale. After a while, she lifted an arm in greeting.

I didn't know when the bed had arrived or who had arranged for its delivery and installation.

Every day involved a single task: taking a bath, changing the sheets, walking a few steps along the corridor. In a few weeks, there would be a round of treatment.

I'd planned to go home once my grandmother was out of the hospital, but then I realized that I couldn't leave the city: our residency permits had expired and our new ones still had not arrived.

Don't worry about it, my mother said, each time I apologized for not being there. We have everything sorted out.

That made me even sadder, as if my arrival had never been expected and they'd never really counted on me to help.

I sent more chocolates and a shawl for my grandmother. In the meantime, relatives and friends brought soups and homemade cakes. Still, my gifts were placed center stage and my grandmother told all the visitors to taste the chocolates. I'd come upon such a scene during a video call, when the downstairs neighbor came over with a tray of fruit.

Just in time to meet Asya, my grandmother said proudly.

The neighbor woman waved in my direction.

Your grandmother always talks about you, she said. Whereas I knew nothing about this woman, not even her name; my mother referred to her as the downstairs neighbor. But I could now see that the three of them were a group of sorts while I was only a guest on-screen. The neighbor had taken a seat at the foot of the bed and was massaging my grandmother's ankles, as naturally as one might stroke a pet, or a child's head. I wanted to tell her to let go. And I had an urge to apologize to them all.

Courtship

I hadn't seen Lena since the exhibition when we parted in bad moods. We'd texted once or twice, but we were both aware that something was off. It was Lena who finally asked me to come to the café after her shift.

I arrived early and took a table outside. Another waitress came to take my order. Lena was by the register, chatting with a young guy. I thought that she looked glowing—a sort of confidence, I assumed, maybe love.

I'd finished my coffee when she came out. She took off the apron tied around her waist, pulled out the pencil holding up her hair and sat in front of me.

It's been ages, she said.

I had prepared myself to act restrained but I was just happy to see her.

I need to talk this whole thing through, Lena said. I guess you know that Ravi and I hung out a few times.

I told her I knew very little beyond that.

Ravi didn't mention it?

Not really.

I thought you guys told each other everything, she said despondently.

So I'd been wrong about Lena's glow of confidence.

She'd written to Ravi after the evening we all dressed up. There was clearly something there, and she hadn't given a second thought to taking the initiative, even though she was usually sensitive to those petty politics. They'd met up a few days later to watch a film. Everything seemed easy between them.

Easy, you know, but not relaxed—he's a pretty anxious type.

They walked for hours. Nothing had happened, not like that, but the attraction couldn't be denied.

I hate being made to believe that I've imagined the whole thing, Lena said.

They met up again, to have lunch and see a show. They ended up skipping the show, because they were enjoying their conversation so much; once again they walked all day. By the end of their following meeting Lena had been so certain of their connection that she'd kissed him. She'd assumed that Ravi was too shy. And that had been that; he hadn't written to her since. Nor had he wanted to come up to her place, Lena added, after the kiss.

It's so confusing, she said. Honestly, it's humiliating.

I'm annoyed with Ravi, I told her. What the hell?

It's making me very nervous, Lena said. I can barely get through a single day.

I suggested going to an afternoon screening. We got tickets to a film about two women living on an island as an act of resistance. We bought chocolate and popcorn and Pepsi. When we came out, it was already dark.

Future Selves

This one was right at the edge of the old town, on the steep hill like a passageway between two different cities.

The staircase smelled of mold, there was no elevator, and the courtyard advertised as an outdoor space was nothing but the trash bins. The real estate agent explained that it would come in handy for a pram. Agents were often presenting to us our future lives with a child. They proposed spare rooms as nurseries, listed schools and daycare centers nearby. They didn't ask about our plans and we didn't say anything to agree with or correct them. There was little to say, after all, as either agreement or correction. An unarticulated tangle in the midst of our lives.

The apartment was old, but more charming than decrepit. Wooden beams crossed the living room ceiling; there was a tiled fireplace in the bedroom, though it was out of use. Still, we could fill the hearth with candles. I had already made a mental arrangement: many white ones of different sizes. I could suddenly see us there, with our own couch and dishes and towels. I wondered whether this was how some women felt about the prospect of having a child: that they could easily imagine a space for it.

Manu asked if I had noticed the view. He pointed to the window, whose ledge was just wide enough to sit on. I pulled up my feet and looked out. The city was creamy and snug and exact. Yes, I thought.

Afterward, we sat down at the closest café and ordered salads. I took out a pen and paper. First, we wrote down all the money we had and all the money we would need. This was not a fun exercise so we started to list all the furniture we would like to buy. A daybed was crucial, I insisted. Manu said we should splurge on one good armchair. And nice lamps, I added. Nice homes always had nice lamps.

Meanwhile, the waitress brought our salads: two bowls of dull lettuce, with canned corn and tuna for topping. The bread basket was copious and a little stale.

I like it here, Manu said, and for whatever reason, I agreed.

Territory

A few days later we met Ravi at an Indian restaurant. It was an unusual spot for us, neither home nor bar. Ravi was the one to suggest it and I felt that he was avoiding our usual intimacies. He'd taken on new students, and had classes on most evenings.

He made his order after a glance at the menu. Any other day, I would have told him he was making a bad choice. Manu would have suggested appetizers to share. But we hadn't quite settled into one another's company.

What's new with you guys? Ravi asked when the waiter left.

We told him about the apartment.

We're thinking of making an offer, Manu said.

That's great, Ravi said. Just go for it. You shouldn't overthink these things.

That doesn't make sense, I told him. We're buying a place to live, with all the money we'll make for the next several decades. We should be doing nothing but over-thinking it.

Geez, Ravi said. Lighten up.

Anyway, I said, aren't you going to tell us what happened?

What're you talking about? Nothing happened.

Come on, man, Manu said.

I'm assuming you're referring to Lena, Ravi said. I mean, we're all adults here.

It was his favorite refrain, whenever he wanted to evade a subject.

Lena seems to think you're avoiding her, I said.

Which is her right, Ravi said.

That's just nonsense, I said.

We had a few good conversations and that's what it is. She's a little intense.

She said the same about you, I snapped.

That's fair, Ravi said. Look, I like hanging out with her but I feel exhausted afterward.

He explained that in her company, every tiny issue could be a matter of scrutiny, every idea questioned to shreds. He had to pick all his words carefully.

For example, I said, in her company you might need to think twice about telling us not to overthink a home purchase.

Ravi put up his hands in arrest.

Sorry, I said. I know what you mean.

After that, we lightened up. Ravi said we should all get together again.

I mean all four of us, he added. That might be fun.

We started listing things Ravi might say at such a gathering that Lena would scrutinize. But this time we were laughing.

Practicality

I saw the Great Dame sitting at her usual spot outside the café and I decided to take the table next to hers. I had dressed up that morning, for no reason except that I'd talked to my grandmother on video. The previous week, she'd said to me:

It makes me feel younger to see you.

It was a shock to be reminded of my youth, which I had recently abandoned. It seemed to belong to another time, when the future happened on its own rather than being shaped by our efforts.

I brushed my hair, put on lipstick, wore my brightest top for the call.

My grandmother talked more steadily than she had since the operation, so I was in high spirits. On my way out of the apartment, I put on a pair of impractical yellow shoes to match my top. Impracticality was its own type of festivity.

The Dame surveyed me from head to toe as I sat down. I smiled at her and she smiled back. She was the one to start a conversation: In all the years that she'd been coming to the café, today was the first time the waiter had brought something sweet with her coffee. It was a real treat, she said. I'd picked a good day.

I told her that I lived close by and came there frequently.

How nice to meet a neighbor, the Dame said. She asked about other places I frequented, where I lived, whether I was acquainted with the stray neighborhood cat. She commented that I had a delightful accent: what place did I consider home? She looked approvingly as I spoke, as if I had thus far provided all the right answers.

My coffee arrived without anything on the side, and the Dame asked the waiter to bring me a cookie as well. I was animated by her attention. I decided to tell her that, besides our neighborhood, we also had our work in common.

Oh really, the Dame said, and suddenly lost interest. She must have expected that I would now tell her about my own films or begin to praise hers, because she turned her chair away from me, facing the street. I realized that the Dame guarded her work with her life. She'd invented a whole new person for such occasions—one that talked about sweet treats and neighborhood cafés. And both of these selves, it seemed to me, were remarkably lonely women.

Principles of Kinship

Perhaps the image of the Dame on the café terrace was not something I wanted, even if I wanted a bit of the Dame's free spirit.

It was the dreadful part of winter, slushing forward to a dreary spring. The city streets were filled with trash. I decided to throw a party.

I invited Lena, Ravi, Sharon and Paul, and some of the new arrivals to the city. I bought more wineglasses and a white platter with splashes of blue. Instead of the Dame's single café table, I wanted a long one crowded with people.

Lena looked different when I opened the door to greet her. She was dressed up, which wasn't unusual, and had makeup on like she often did. Still, she appeared strange. It was her formality, I realized, as if she had arrived for a job interview.

I hugged her and she asked where Ravi was.

On his way probably. I shrugged.

I'd spent the whole afternoon cooking and I was upset with Manu that he hadn't proposed coming home early from work, to help. I guessed that he found the gathering excessive, making a feast for so many people we weren't even close to. We could have met up at a bar, he'd said, and I didn't tell him about the image of the long table, why it mattered to me.

I'd cooked more food than was necessary. There were dips, bowls of grains, plates of smoked fish and meats. On the new platter with splashes of blue, I stacked vegetables of every color. I had also made dishes that resembled my and Manu's native cuisines, even though we never ate these types of things.

When Ravi arrived, he greeted Lena briefly, before joining another conversation. Lena came up to me.

You're such a good housewife, she said.

It was the sort of comment she and I would have laughed about, but I didn't find it funny after a day of cooking. In fact, I was finding it harder to laugh with Lena. She could probably sense this because she was all the more sarcastic.

I went over to Sharon who was talking about their recent renovation: a faucet, old plumbing, broken tiles. I was grateful to be part of the conversation without having to participate; I suddenly wanted nothing more than to be alone and lie on the couch.

Years ago, after we graduated and were renting our first apartment, we were surrounded by people who entered our lives for a few days, many of whom we never saw again. We hosted friends of friends who needed a place to stay, ended up at dinners with people we didn't know. Back then, it felt perfectly normal. We didn't make an effort to become friends with these strangers, but we were always curious to hear what they had to say. From time to time, we would remember one of these people we'd put up on a couch, and we marveled at our energy and enthusiasm. At that time, we owned only two pillows; we would give one of our own to our guest and sleep on a folded sweater. We didn't have many routines and didn't mind the disruption of order. We would sit up late with these strangers talking about their lives, their interests—we must have been too young to talk about our work, though we always had plenty to say about what we thought we wanted to do, what we believed adamantly were our passions. Nor did we think that conversations with these strangers were useless just because they weren't going to establish a community. Back then, it was still me and Manu behind our curtain, at a remove from the world. There wasn't the worry of making things sturdy. At night, we'd offer the strangers drinks and snacks. In the mornings, we made elaborate breakfasts, though we had little money to spare. Whenever we talked about this time in our lives, we would be incredulous at our hospitality but also a bit mournful at our loss of curiosity. Our tolerance to listen to anything, to be engaged with the world without calculation.

Meanwhile, Sharon was continuing her story about the renovations. I now wanted these people to stick around, even if I had no interest in what they were saying.

Lena had taken a seat on the couch and was surveying the room coolly. There was something daring in the way she looked perfectly at ease, not joining any conversation, as if she were calling us out.

The Mirror

Lena phoned a few days later.

Did you manage to clean up? she asked. With all that food.

Will you stop making the same joke?

Who said I was joking?

Are things better between you and Ravi?

They're okay, she said, shedding her sarcasm. I think he was embarrassed of me at the party.

I told her she was imagining that. I wasn't trying to dismiss her. I was just desperate for things to be harmonious.

When I recounted the party to my mother, I told her about the way Lena had sat alone in a corner watching everyone. It was as if, I said, she set out to spoil any situation that appeared decent, because she found decency offensive. But I knew I hadn't managed to describe the heart of the matter. And now my mother had taken arms against Lena and told me to keep my distance.

No, it's nothing like that, I backpedaled. I'm not saying she's deranged or anything.

Still, my mother said, it's not worth the agitation.

I just wanted to have a nice gathering, I went on. I spent all day cooking.

Sweetheart, my mother said, next time just meet up at a restaurant.

I described the situation to my grandmother as well, this time with more generosity.

It was as if, I said, Lena could spot insincerity before anyone else and could not pretend afterward that she hadn't seen it.

Some people, my grandmother said mysteriously, are born holding a mirror to the world. But, she added, I shouldn't get too involved in my friends' unhappiness.

My mother and grandmother were always telling me to focus on my own life. I agreed with them, but I didn't quite know where my life began and how far it extended. I didn't want to risk cutting off any vital parts.

Thresholds

The door was open. We went in, shouting hello. We'd brought a roast chicken and a pear tart. Tereza wasn't in the kitchen or the living room. We called out to her.

Yes? Tereza called back. Who is it?

She was sitting at the edge of the bed in her nightgown.

What a surprise, she exclaimed, and we didn't remind her that we had planned to have dinner.

We just stopped by to ask if you wanted to eat together, Manu said.

It's a party, my friends, Tereza said. I helped her put on a sweater.

In the kitchen, Manu and I began setting the table.

Tereza, I said, do you lock the door when you come home from a walk?

Always, she responded. You never know who'll sneak into the home of an old croak.

Manu raised his eyebrows at me.

We sat on either side of Tereza. She didn't eat any chicken but she had two slices of tart. Afterward, she offered us chocolates that she brought from her bedroom.

They're very good for you, she said, holding out the box, which was mostly empty. Then we went to the living room and sat in front of the television. Manu switched channels until he arrived at the classical music.

Here they are, Tereza said, and began narrating everything we could see for ourselves.

There's the lovely violin player with long black hair. Here's the cellist. Here comes the conductor.

When the music started, she reached her hands left and right and held our wrists. We sat through the concert while Tereza dozed off.

That night, smoking a joint, we considered telling Tereza's daughter about the open door.

She can't really live alone, Manu said.

It's just one time, I said. Everyone can be forgetful.

What if something happened?

But what if the daughter puts her in a home?

That would be so depressing.

Exactly.

Anyway, Manu said, she already knows that Tereza's mind wanders a little.

Right, I said.

Present Tense

I was scrolling through the footage on my camera on a Sunday morning. I looked up when I heard the sound of the vacuum cleaner. Manu was pushing and pulling on the carpet with his headphones on. I suddenly saw what a gentle dance this was, his weekly waltz around our home, back and forth, out to the corners and back to center. I turned on the camera to film him. Manu didn't notice me. He must have been listening to the history podcast that transported him, on any given week, to a different place. This was one reason for Manu's calm optimism, because he was constantly immersed in narratives of creation and collapse, centuries condensed to the span of forty-five minutes, from which he emerged, taking off his headphones, a little transformed, back in the present world, which was no more or less strange than the one he'd just traveled to. He would summarize what he'd learned to me during walks, about the Sumerians,

Assyrians, Mayans, Etruscans, and Olmecs; Siberian shamans and Baltic crusaders; skull mutilation and ritual cannibalism; the Opium Wars and the craze for tulips. I retained only bits of information from his retellings, not because I wasn't interested, but because I felt assured that he was learning these things for both of us and that I could consult him whenever I wanted, like certain books I wished to have in our library, even if I didn't intend to read them, because they provided comfort in their silent knowledge.

Meanwhile on my camera screen, Manu unplugged the vacuum and plugged it again to the wall on the other side of the living room. He was like the people at the park, I thought, immersed in the calm of the day.

Posterity

I told my grandmother I wanted to film her the next time I visited. I'd always known her talon-grip on life, so I couldn't understand her response.

What do you have to film me for?

You're full of stories, I said, because I couldn't tell her the real reason.

And you look great on camera, I went on. Also, I want us to make something together.

There's nothing to tell, my grandmother said.

What about the time you played the lead role in Molière?

The mayor brought roses to the stage.

And all the papers wrote about it.

That's right.

We can start there.

What else is there to say?

Grandma, I said, you're a queen.

That's all over now, she said. You should focus on your own work.

Then she called out to my mother, and without warning passed her the phone.

Grandma is a bit sleepy, my mother said. We'll call you later, sweetheart.

Family Archive

For our appointment with the bank, Manu put on his white shirt and I put on a dress and cardigan. I suggested wearing our wedding rings, which we'd discarded a few months into our marriage. Manu's made him itch; mine was too loose on my finger. Manu said it was unnecessary to wear our rings, the type of thing you saw in movies, when witnesses had to dress up to look trustworthy. In reality, such things were unlikely to make a difference, he thought. Even so, I insisted that we should do our best to look like people who would pay off a mortgage.

The banker—or was he called a financial consultant?—greeted us busily at the door then told us to wait while he finished something else. He thumbed through papers, clicked on his screen, stacked documents.

Here we are then, he finally announced, looking up. He must have been younger than us but he had the manners of a primary school teacher, or a seasoned waiter.

We see that Madam is a freelance earner?

From his expression, we could tell this was a troubling type of earner to be.

Let's see if we can manage something, he said. He dragged the bars of simulation on his screen, up and down, frowning. I will have to make a case to my bosses, he said. It won't be simple but I'll try.

He asked us to send him a list of documents and we told him we would do so quickly.

On our way back, I told Manu that our efforts to appear respectable had worked. The banker had believed our good intentions, despite our incomes. Manu was skeptical.

It's his job to make it look like he's doing us a grand favor, he said. We're the ones devoting the considerable remainder of our lives paying off the mortgage.

Anyway, it's good that we met with a banker, I said. I feel very adult.

Technically, Manu said, I think he's called something else. But he couldn't think of the word.

At home, we went through our documents, all of them stuffed into two bulging manila envelopes, tearing at the seams, buried in the bottom drawer of my desk beneath batteries, the charger for a camera I no longer used, a bag of coins accumulated from travels. Each time I proposed throwing it away, Manu would tell me that this was actually illegal, and I would say nothing back, and the topic would be adjourned for another few months or a year, until I looked at the drawer in despair and suggested getting rid of the useless bag of metal.

While the various nests of chaos in the apartment bothered us whenever we were reminded of their existence, the torn manila envelopes stuffed beyond capacity continued to make sense to us: if we needed to find an important document, we knew that it could only be in one of the two envelopes. They contained our birth and marriage certificates, insurance cards, past visas and passports, bank statements, apartment lease, medical forms, printouts of visa applications, the exoskeletons of passport photos with only a single picture remaining. There were also the pay stubs I'd received in the past two years teaching documentary techniques, and it was these that we were now sorting through, in order to put together a respectable story of my income. Still, we could not stitch certain gaps—from October to March, and another year, from November to January.

Where else might you have put them? Manu asked, trying not to show his exasperation, though we had now been looking for two days.

Nowhere else.

Could you have thrown them out?

I don't think so.

On the phone, I told my mother that we were assembling a portfolio for a loan application.

I can't believe it, my mother said. I would never have expected it of the two of you.

Our families had a foundational myth of me and Manu that was different from our own. My mother believed that our love for each other had something to do with the way that we tolerated each other's mess and procrastination, even enabled it. For my father it was the fact that we lived so modestly, with a great tolerance for discomfort. He couldn't understand why our couch was so narrow, our bathroom so cramped, our meals so meager. For Manu's parents, we were united in our love of old things. The first time they visited us in the city, soon after we'd moved into our apartment—which we'd furnished with a farm table, a chest of drawers, a wardrobe, and a record player—they said that the place was like the village homes of a century ago. It wasn't a compliment. To them, old things did not have the charm they did for us. Aged objects pointed to hardship, to ways of life they did not need to romanticize, because they had experienced them firsthand. Their own home resembled the lobby of a three-star hotel.

On our third day of searching, we found the pay slips for the missing months. They were tucked away inside a smaller envelope that contained the results of an eye exam and prescriptions for contact lenses.

We scanned all the documents and sent them to the bank. A week later, we received an email about what the bank could loan us. It was much less than the amount we'd been told at the meeting, and I guessed that the banker had not succeeded in making a case to his superiors, after all.

With that number, we made an offer on the apartment with the wooden beams and out-of-service fireplace and the window nook with a view. Since our visit, it had retained its charm, whereas other places faded in our memory soon after we saw them, quickly seeming like lives that weren't ours. We'd talked about all the things that would remain the same if we moved to the beamed apartment: we could still walk to the beer bar where we met Ravi, I would take the same metro line to Lena's café. We would be a bus ride away from the flea market. When listed like this, it seemed as if we had a real life in the city—places to go, people to see.

We flipped through the photographs on Manu's telephone. We enlarged the photo of the window nook for closer inspection; we passed quickly when we came to the picture of the old bathroom. A nice bathroom, after all, was not a priority but a luxury, we said.

The estate agent told us he would get back to us about our offer.

In the Park

Here in front of the greenhouses is my favorite spot. When the sun's out, you pull up a chair and sit alongside the others. We're a community of sun worshippers. We recognize one another. We take pleasure in each other's basking. The true baskers don't do anything at all. You see? No books, no newspapers, no phones. Only the sun. This year, I didn't go on holiday, but just look at me. It's like I spent months on the Mediterranean.

Principles of Kinship

There was another party at Sharon and Paul's, so we had the same argument.

Didn't we just see them? Manu said.

Is there a quota?

But we don't even like them.

I like them, I said. I don't dislike them. They're annoying and pretentious and sweet. Just like cousins.

But they're not our cousins, Manu said.

It didn't quite make sense, all this over a simple party. There must have been more to it, but we didn't break the surface.

Ravi and Lena were going, too.

On the day of the party, Lena called to ask what I'd wear.

I don't know, I told her, which wasn't exactly true. Nothing fancy, I added.

I feel strange around that group, Lena said. It's like they're all part of some club.

One time, Lena had told me that she could identify at a glance people who had transformed in life. Those who had become more beautiful, more educated, wealthier. It was the lingering insecurity that gave them away, she said, which others often mistook for modesty. Whereas the modesty of truly secure people was in fact a type of arrogance, a certainty about their life and its place in the greater scheme of things.

They must think the same about us, I told her without conviction.

The four of us arrived together, with wine and flowers, which was probably unnecessary. As soon as we entered, Ravi announced that he would stay only an hour or so.

Come on, man, I said, mostly for Lena's sake. Just play along.

Everyone's free to leave, Ravi said.

So much for the drinking spirit, I jabbed, and Ravi ignored me.

Like the previous visit, Izzy was allowed to charm the guests for a short time, after which she was handed an iPad.

Enlightened parenting, Lena whispered to me, and I nodded quickly in recognition, hoping she wouldn't continue.

Sharon was walking around the room, showering the guests with compliments. Everyone was a beauty, a genius, a darling.

She introduced Manu to a man who looked like he had arrived at the wrong place, and led me by the arm toward an older woman.

You two must talk, she told us, before stepping away. It wasn't entirely clear why she wanted us to talk. It seemed rather that she didn't want to sacrifice her own time to the task.

Once we'd exchanged names, the woman launched into a description of her past work as a conservator at a museum. She talked urgently, even though she was retired. She responded hastily to my remarks—a painting I loved for its colors, a room where I liked to sit and read—then continued her monologue.

From the corner of my eye, I saw that Manu had already abandoned his companion and was sitting with Ravi on the couch at the back of the room.

I told the woman I would go get some food.

Great idea, she said, following me.

Maybe I wasn't so wrong in thinking that the hosts were like our cousins. After all, we had been paired with the most cumbersome guests. Surely this signaled a familiarity of sorts.

Just as he'd warned us, Ravi was the first to leave. I overheard Lena proposing to come with him; Ravi told her that she should stay and enjoy herself. I felt sad for Lena, and uncomfortable at the thought that I might be responsible. I'd finally abandoned the conservator as well, and I joined Sharon, who was drinking whiskey in the kitchen with some others.

There you are, she said. I hope you didn't mind her company. She's actually quite fascinating.

We got along, I told her.

Oh goodie, Sharon said. I had a feeling you would.

I left the kitchen and found Lena. I told her we could walk together to the metro, if she wanted to leave.

Sure, she said. I'm ready to go.

We went to the bedroom to look for our coats. Izzy was asleep on her parents' bed, still dressed in her party outfit, hugging the iPad.

He's so hard to read, Lena said. I constantly feel like I'm getting on his nerves.

I didn't know what to tell her, so I pretended to be engrossed in the search for my scarf.

Light

Another one of Manu, in black and white, out of some recognition for the early morning. The radio is on. It's the end of the news. Then there is music, something like a chant, soothing and repetitive. Manu knows I'm filming him but doesn't mind, or doesn't care. Anyway he's used to it. Some part of his face is hidden by the computer screen, which reflects its light on his cheekbones, puffy with sleep. It's a weekend. He is wearing the old shirt I bought him when we first met, with the silhouette of a blackbird.

What're you doing? I ask.

He looks up from the screen.

Just a quick game of chess.

He returns to his game. On the radio, a rock song comes on, one we both listened to in our own teenage bedrooms. Manu looks up again.

I can't believe they're playing this, he says. Then he says:

What time should we have breakfast?

Now sunshine is streaming through the window. The table, and Manu's face, are bright with light.

Pity for the Old

Manu and I were at the supermarket when the real estate agent called to tell us our offer on the apartment was accepted. We would get together with the current owners the following week. We paid for the milk and bananas in the basket and went out, forgetting about everything else we needed to buy.

Are you happy about it? Manu asked.

If you are.

When we came home, which smelled faintly of last evening's cooking, my eyes welled with tears.

Our little home, Manu said, and the tears began rolling down my cheeks.

We stood looking at the living room, crammed with our life. Already, we had discussed leaving most of these things behind when we moved. The artworks would be more refined, the furnishings statelier and few in number. But it seemed now like a betrayal.

A few days later we walked to the new apartment to meet the owner. It took us forty-five minutes, through one beautiful neighborhood and one desolate. As we got closer, we picked out the places we would frequent in our new lives, even though we knew these initial enthusiasms never played out as expected. When we first moved to the city, we'd spotted a noodle shop down the street from us, where we had imagined becoming regulars, having our order known without asking. But we'd still never eaten there. Now we walked past it with some sort of shame, as if it were witness to how little we had managed to make the city our own.

The hallway smelled more strongly of mold than we remembered. We went up the four flights of stairs, this time paying attention to the toll of the climb.

At the door, the real estate agent shook both our hands.

The first time is always special, he said.

The owner was seated at the dining table, reading glasses propped on her nose, scrolling her phone. She was around the same age as my mother. In fact, she looked a bit like my mother. She got up slowly and held out her hand, though not so much in congratulation.

There are some snacks, she announced pointing to a tray. There was one miniature muffin and one biscuit for each of us, as if the owner did not want to overdo her hospitality. We sat around the table and complimented her on her apartment.

I bought it on a whim many years ago, she told us. She lived outside the city and came here for concerts, dinners with friends. But recently, it had become difficult to visit as often as she would like and the small apartment was starting to feel wasteful.

She didn't ask us any questions but we still told her enthusiastically about our first visit, how we loved the window nook, how much this place would suit our lives.

I thought she considered it a little pathetic that we were buying her weekend home to live in. But I also noticed, beneath the condescension, some tenderness toward us, curiosity for our lives ahead, and perhaps some memory of a past life.

In the Park

I asked Ravi for a park interview.

As the token foreigner? he said, but he agreed.

We met up by the lake. It was early evening, the water silvery and smooth. Manu would join us there after work. I set up the camera on a tripod, taking my time because I was feeling a little awkward.

Why don't you tell me why you come to the park and we'll go from there, I proposed.

Okay, Ravi said, looking very stiff.

I fumbled with the camera settings so he could take some time to settle. I often started shooting this way, making it look like I was adjusting something, while my subjects assumed their natural states.

I guess I come here most often with you guys, Ravi began. But sometimes I come on my own in the afternoon. First I walk the whole periphery. It feels like a waste to come to the park and not see it in full. I worry about wasting the day. I don't mean productivity, I just mean enjoying it.

No, I'm not against productivity. But you have to define it on your own terms.

It never feels wasteful to come to the park. But in the end, it's the people that make a place. I could live anywhere with the right people.

Yeah, I do mean that. Even if I like to be alone a lot of the time.

No, I don't think I'm very private, I just don't see the point of sharing everything. I don't think in those terms. There's nothing attractive about disclosing everything to everyone, even to yourself. There has to be some mystery.

Where do I feel most like myself? I don't know how to answer that question. I guess I'm still looking.

Rupture

Please go up to my mother's, Tereza's daughter pleaded on the phone.

Some weeks ago, she'd asked Tereza to give us a set of keys in case of emergency. And here it was.

Tereza was on the kitchen floor, one arm propped underneath.

Oh, Tereza, I said.

She looked at us, sweet and mute like a parrot, with her round bright eyes.

The ambulance was on its way, and we didn't dare move her. We sat on either side of her, holding her hands. At some point, she threw up without a sound and we wiped her face and sweater.

I was holding back from saying the types of things one might say to a child, cooing and soothing and hushing. There was our friendship at stake, the way we read poems together. Even now, we had to hold on to our codes of conduct rather than abandoning them to the crisis.

Intention and Design

Practically speaking, we needed to arrange movers, set up internet and electricity, but mostly we went through various drawers, loosening the photographs stuck together, leafing through notebooks, discovering museum tickets.

Sara was coming again—this time for a meeting. She would first stay at a hotel close to her work, then stay with us for one night. I told her our apartment was a mess—boxes in the hallway, the living room half packed up.

I don't mind, she said. We can have dinner out.

Tell Ravi, she added. I'd love to see him.

We met in the early evening at a restaurant. Ravi and Manu were going to join later, so Sara and I could catch up. Lena was at her mother's that evening. I was glad not to have to leave her out, or invite her and worry that she might act strangely. And I understood that she might have gotten in the way on this particular occasion.

Sara ordered a cocktail, I got a beer.

What a treat, Sara said.

I told her about the new apartment: The first time we saw it, I said, I could imagine our belongings inside, I could imagine a life. And when we visited the apartment again, I'd walked in to see my own mother sitting at the dining table. But maybe, I said, the woman looked like me in the future. It sounded more supernatural than it had actually been.

I have goose bumps, Sara said. What a story.

I'd omitted the owner's haughtiness and her look of envy, as well as the state of the building, worse than we remembered.

When Ravi and Manu arrived, Sara said that the story of our encounter with our home was truly mystical. They looked a bit puzzled, but I didn't explain further.

So, Sara asked Ravi. Have you kept the drinking spirit alive in my absence? I was happy that she remembered and I also felt worried about what I'd initiated.

These two can deflate the spirit, Ravi said. I was awaiting your return.

During dinner, he avoided any subject that might relate to Lena. When Sara went to the bathroom, I asked if he knew when Lena was coming back from her mother's. Ravi shrugged.

You'd know better, he said.

You haven't talked to her?

Not really.

What're we having for dessert? Sara asked when she returned. Let's get everything to share.

I really need to move to this city, she went on. I mean, the company is mediocre but the food is outstanding.

I wanted to be at the park at sunrise the next morning. I was going to film the unlocking of the gates. I'd told Sara this when we planned the dinner.

Maybe we should get going, I said.

What did I just tell you, about their drinking spirit? Ravi said.

You go ahead, Sara said. I'd like to walk around for a bit, get a nightcap.

I gave Sara my set of keys. We might be asleep by the time she got back, I told her. But her bed was ready and I'd be back from the park before she left for her train.

I won't make a sound, she said, and kissed me on the cheek. See you tomorrow.

On the metro, Manu and I discussed the possibility of Ravi and Sara.

It's a distinct possibility, Manu said.

What about Lena?

That's Ravi's problem.

It puts us in an uncomfortable position.

It puts *him* in an uncomfortable position.

I'm the reason they're hanging out.

Then you shouldn't have invited him tonight.

What're you saying?

You were upset when Ravi started flirting with Lena, now you're upset because he's flirting with Sara. And you were the one who set it up both times.

That's a strange way to put it, I told him. I thought things would go more smoothly.

You get so worried about these things, he said. It's their life.

But it was our life, too. We had started from scratch and we were just laying down the foundation.

In the morning, Sara's bed was untouched. When I returned from the park some hours later, she texted that she was already at the train station. She'd had a really nice evening, she wrote. It was such a treat to see me. While I was thinking about what to write back to her, she added that she had left the keys with Ravi. She sent another message following this, of a monkey covering its face with its hands.

Haha, I typed, not knowing what else to say.

Visiting Hours

The hospital room was filled with people, chatting among themselves while Tereza looked around in a daze.

She had broken her hip when she fell. She was wearing her nightgown, surrounded by flowers.

How sweet of you to come, Tereza's daughter told us. These are my mother's neighbors, she announced. They've been so helpful.

Some people nodded in our direction. We didn't know any of them, and it seemed that we were witnessing a real order that had so far eluded us, that our dinners with Tereza were make believe, at best.

We went up to Tereza's bed.

Manu took out a book of poems from his bag and put it by the flowers.

You've got great style, Tereza told him.

Mama, her daughter said, isn't it lovely that your neighbors came?

She told us they were all just stepping out for lunch. We were welcome to stay for as long as we liked.

We sat with Tereza, on either side of her bed. She rocked her face from side to side, smiling at us. Manu leafed through the book and read out a poem, even though Tereza looked like she had fallen asleep.

The poem was about the sky. The greatness of it, and fickleness. Clouds drifted, the sky darkened, the moon appeared.

Tereza opened her eyes. You know, she said, it's very curious.

What's curious, Tereza? I asked, but she'd lost her train of thought. Still, her eyes were as bright as ever.

The Documentarian

Lena was over on her day off, soon after Manu left for work.

The apartment was mostly packed up, except for a few cups and plates. The walls had bright white squares where there had been frames. The light had so much space to fill.

I was working on the documentary when Lena arrived. She looked at the still image of the carousel on my computer screen and asked to see a few minutes. I was excited by the prospect; I'd been wondering how the footage would appear to an outsider. I was ready to open it up for viewing, to step out of my own mind.

I made a pot of coffee. We sat at the dining table with the computer in front of us.

Lena's face remained expressionless as she watched. After a while, I shut the laptop closed.

That's all I have for now, I said self-consciously.

What will you do next? Lena asked.

The question threw me off. I thought she might have offered some thoughts, if not a bit of encouragement.

I guess I'll continue filming?

Lena didn't comment. I asked if she wanted more coffee.

I heard your friend was visiting, Lena said.

Earlier that morning, I'd texted Ravi that Lena was coming over, in case he wanted to tell me anything.

Great, Ravi wrote back. How's the packing coming along?

She was only here one night, I told Lena. We had dinner together. Ravi was there, too.

I know, Lena said. He was all fishy about it.

Lena was especially beautiful that day, sitting at the table. Her skin was luminous, as if lit through with fever.

So, Lena said, why's he being so fishy?

You two need to figure out how to speak to each other without all this roundabout investigation.

It's a shame, she said. I didn't even get to know him.

But you do know him, I said, awkwardly. It's good old Ravi.

I guess you're not going to tell me, Lena said.

There's nothing to tell, I said, sounding a lot like Ravi. We went out for dinner and Sara went back the next morning. I would have invited you but you were at your mother's.

I'm assuming something happened between them.

Why do you think that? I asked.

At first, I had the feeling that Ravi was mocking me, she said. Now, I have the feeling that you're in on it, too.

Of course not, I told her. I just don't want to take sides.

There's always a side, Lena said.

Ways to Live

For now, the film started with the merry-go-round man lifting the metal curtains to reveal the horse and carriage and fire truck. I transitioned to the old women moving their arms and legs slowly on the grass; teenagers on benches; a pregnant woman walking the outer edge. All of them immersed in the day, the green serenity.

The foliage and flowers and light shifted; so did the clothes of the park natives, layering, then shedding. The empty stretches of frosted grass were littered with bare limbs as spring turned to summer.

An old man said that he'd resided all his life in one of the buildings facing the park. As a child, his parents would take him here every weekend to walk around the lake and eat an ice cream. The ice cream vendors were no longer allowed inside the gates, he said. He had seen so much change. But he still recognized the great plane trees and cedars of his childhood. And now that he had little to do with his days and no one to take care of, he came to the park daily to check up on them. I hadn't known, when I was filming, with what sort of emotion he'd said all this. I only noticed while editing that his eyes were sparkling with tears. From him I moved to Ravi, his words whittled down to match the old man's in their gentle mystery.

All the months that I had been filming, I'd thought that there were so many ways of living, of inhabiting the park. I wanted to know as many configurations as possible, all the strange and unique ways. But lately, as I went over the scenes again and again, smoothing their edges, positioning them into a fluid conversation, I'd begun to understand that there was, also, only one way to live beneath the multitude of forms, one way forward through the fleeting hours of a day.

Thresholds

Tereza came back from the hospital with a woman who would live with her from then on. We ran into them in front of the building. Tereza's daughter and the helper were trying to get Tereza out of the car and into her wheelchair. Her hip would take time to heal. But worse, the daughter told us, was that her mind was more muddled now than ever.

Hello, darlings, Tereza called out to us. Is this a party or what?

She talks nonsense, the daughter said. Constantly.

She was desperate for us to understand this. Perhaps it was the necessary preparation for a parent's death. But I didn't want to think more about what this meant.

Manu and I introduced ourselves to the caretaker who hadn't yet said a word. Her name was Anya. We told her we would be seeing her around, for dinners that were also poetry readings. We hadn't yet told Tereza that we were moving. And I guessed that we would probably never do so. We'd go over for dinners, we would visit often. Tereza might not notice any change. It seemed easier this way. There was no need to cause her sadness, or confusion. To make her feel that her world was changing.

Anya stared at us blankly.

Tereza, I said, how nice that you'll have a friend at home.

Oh? Tereza said. You must meet my lovely neighbors.

I didn't say anything more, fearing I might prove the daughter right.

Intimacy

When we got the keys to the new apartment, Ravi came to see it. We were moving out in two weeks and we had done very little in the form of practicalities. There was no hot water or internet. The radiators sputtered some liquid and remained ice cold. There were no hooks for towels, no sponges to clean the counters, no rollers or brushes for the tub of white paint we had bought. In fact, we didn't know what else we might need to paint a wall.

Ravi walked through the rooms without saying anything. With the previous owner's furniture gone, the place looked a little smaller, and dirtier.

It's great, he finally said. It's exactly where I imagined you living.

I felt offended that he likened the place to us, without having seen what it would become. And honestly, it didn't look very nice to me, right then. For a moment, I thought we'd made a very big change for no reason at all. But I wasn't going to tell Manu that. Anyway, he'd probably figured it out for himself.

We discussed where the table should go, and what sort of bookshelves we could put up. We took measurements of the walls, though we had nothing in mind regarding these lengths and heights. Still, it felt good to be there with Ravi, playing at being practical. It seemed so much like the right direction.

I'd noticed that Ravi was wearing something around his neck. A long piece of string, with something like a stone hanging from the end: I couldn't see clearly because it was hidden beneath his shirt. I thought this was a little unusual; I couldn't imagine him buying himself a necklace. He had a horror of vanity. But for some reason, I couldn't bring myself to ask about it.

After we left the apartment, we went to the beer bar.

You guys know that spot in the park, between the two trees? Ravi said. Where we usually sit? It would be cool to put up a hammock there.

Could be our summer spot, Manu said.

That's what I was thinking, Ravi said.

He ran his fingers along the string of his necklace.

What is that? Manu asked.

A pendant, Ravi said.

Where's it from?

Just a present.

Is it a *secret*? I asked impatiently.

Why would it be? Ravi said. But he didn't give it up.

And so? Manu asked.

It's just something Sara sent.

Ooooo, Manu said. *Ro*-mance.

I guess she makes stuff like this, Ravi said. You'd know better.

No, I told him, I didn't.

In the Park

Next weekend was sunny and we went to the park. Everyone there was giddy with spring.

Ravi had brought the hammock, which belonged to his landlord. Manu and I brought beer and chips. The two trees were too close together so we wandered around looking for a better spot. Once we'd put it up, Ravi climbed in.

This is so great, he said. This is the way to live.

And then he said, I might be done with the city.

Oh yeah? I asked but I didn't take him seriously.

We should all move to the country at some point, Manu said sleepily. He was lying down by the tree trunk.

I mean soon, Ravi said. I spoke with a few schools. There are some interesting options.

What do you mean? Manu said.

Sara thought it might be interesting to give it a go.

Will you stop saying *interesting*? I said.

Wait, Manu said, you're moving away?

I mean, at some point, Ravi said.

Manu propped himself up on his elbows. Ravi, man, can you give us a straight answer?

Okay, Ravi said, I have a job offer. And Sara says I could stay with her for a bit and see how things go.

When did all this happen? I asked. Why didn't you tell us?

I'm telling you, Ravi said. It happened sort of quickly. Sara wanted to talk to you, too. I said I'd bring it up first.

None of the objections that came to mind seemed fair to speak aloud. But I wondered about the hammock—how he'd said it should be our summer spot.

Instead I asked if he had spoken to Lena. For a moment Ravi looked like he was going to object to the question

Yeah, he said after a while. I spoke to her.

You told her you were moving?

I did.

And about Sara?

Yes, I told her.

What did she say?

She was angry, Ravi said. She was really, really angry. She seemed to think we had some kind of agreement.

He looked like a child then. And I thought he looked a bit scared.

A few days later, Sharon called me on the phone.

Have you been in touch with your friend Lena? she asked.

I told her I hadn't.

She's a piece of work, Sharon said. I mean, she is totally nuts.

The previous afternoon, Sharon was in a part of town she never went to, because she had an appointment with her gynecologist. Afterward, she went into a café to treat herself—she hated these checkups—where she ran into Lena.

I guess she works there? Sharon said. I didn't realize she worked at a café.

I was going to ask why that mattered, but I didn't want to interrupt. I was starting to feel uneasy.

So, are you having more of your *parties* these days? Lena asked.

Just the way she spoke, Sharon said. It was so weird.

Sure, Sharon told her, you're always invited.

That's so kind of you, Lena said. And then she said suddenly that they were totally dull. Their whole "show." The way they all pretended to be such interesting people.

I'm telling you exactly what she said, Sharon said to me. This crazy woman told me, *All you people ever do is find ways to stifle your boredom.* And she didn't even take my order.

Oh my, I told Sharon. That doesn't sound good.

She'd even gone off about their parenting, the way they had brought a child into the world only to station her in front of a screen and get on with their lives.

Can you believe it? Sharon asked.

I told her I couldn't. I also felt, with panic, that I might not be able to contain my laughter.

But do you know what's wrong with her?

No. I really don't.

In the evening, I recounted all this to Manu.

Wow, he said. Lena's lost it.

Do you think we should call her?

That doesn't sound like a great idea.

But she must be angry with us as well, I said. She must be so angry with me.

That's why it's not a good idea.

I feel so bad for her, I said. But even as I said it, I knew that I was only easing my conscience. And I really did understand what Lena had said, about there always being a side.

Fear of the Old

I saw the fall as I was crossing the street, right in front of the café. There was a loud thud; the old woman's shopping cart spilled all across the pavement. Then a bewildered cry, like a child. By the time I crossed to the other side, others had gathered around the old woman, who was sobbing. Two waiters from the café were trying to give her water. A young woman was collecting the spilled groceries. Someone was cursing the state of the pavements. From Tereza's fall, I knew what number to call and how to describe the situation efficiently. I reached for my phone. It was a good gathering; there was a feeling of love in the air.

After a while, we managed to lift the woman up and walked her to a table outside. We told her the ambulance was on its way.

Oh no, the old woman said. She had stopped sobbing. No need to cause them trouble.

We insisted she couldn't go home alone.

No one knows what's damaged in there, one of the waiters said, tapping his head.

My neighbor's here, the old woman said. I'll just walk back with her.

She pointed behind her. It was the Great Dame, sitting at her usual table. She hadn't shown any interest in the scene unraveling right in front of her; she seemed engrossed in her bread and butter. Once we were all staring at her, she nodded that she was, indeed, the old woman's neighbor.

We'll go home together, the old woman said cheerfully. It'll do us both good. At our age, we need each other's company.

I saw something like anger in the Great Dame's face. Or was it horror? I understood that, like the rest of us, she was terrified her life was passing her by.

Notions of Loyalty

It was a bit curious that I rarely spoke to my grandmother about Tereza. After all, they were around the same age and a similar sort of spark kept them both going. I guess I didn't want to tell my grandmother about the friendship, how often we saw each other, our inside jokes, how we could be up at Tereza's in a minute if we were needed. My grandmother wouldn't have said it, but I still imagined her reproach: what about your own grandmother?

After Tereza came back from the hospital, I told my grandmother about our upstairs neighbor who'd had a terrible fall. It was one of our calls when I had dressed up and put on lipstick. After the surgery, I told my grandmother, there seemed to be something off with our neighbor's mind.

As I said this, I silently apologized to Tereza and I hoped that she would understand why I was betraying her like this.

My grandmother was completely engaged in the story. She moved closer to the screen so I could only see her mouth.

What happened to her mind? she asked.

Well, I said, when she was talking to us, she mentioned that we should meet her downstairs neighbors.

And she meant you? my grandmother shouted.

Yes.

Oh, poor woman, my grandmother said, giddy with excitement. Poor old granny.

Principles of Kinship

It was our last days in our apartment and we had only a pot and a small frying pan so we had simple dinners and sometimes watched two episodes in a row before we continued packing the last remaining things that nevertheless didn't seem to end. We had arranged for movers to arrive early one morning the following week. They would finish by noon.

Manu had been in a bad mood. One evening after we washed the dishes and dried them, he went to the bedroom and lay down to read. I followed him a few minutes later.

Is everything okay? I asked.

Yeah, he said. I'm fine.

But something's up, I said, even though Manu didn't like being probed.

I'm okay, Manu said.

I lay down next to him.

Are you worried about the move?

I think we're on track, he said.

Is it your brother?

I guess, maybe.

Manu, I said, what is it? You're making me nervous.

Don't be nervous, he said. Everything's fine.

I put my hand on his. Manu, I said, we're the *T*s.

That's right.

He pushed himself up and crossed his legs.

I'm upset with Ravi.

That he's moving?

Yes. I mean, so suddenly. It's irrational, but it still feels like a betrayal.

I know what you mean, I told him, because I really did. But I was surprised to hear Manu say it.

He's like family, Manu said. I keep thinking he didn't consider us. It was so easy for him to just leave.

I felt so sorry, then, just like I did on Manu's birthday. For our life together—the smallness of it, however large.

Two days later we met Ravi at the flea market but we were all of us without purpose. That is to say, we'd lost our purposeless ease around those stalls. Manu and I didn't want anything new to add to the boxes. And Ravi didn't even seem to be looking. We went to the dingy bar and ordered the usual pitcher of wine.

Man, Manu said. I just can't believe you're leaving.

I know, crazy, Ravi said.

You seem so chill about it, Manu said. We're going to miss you.

I'll miss you guys, too! Ravi said. I could see this made Manu upset.

We're a little shocked you're leaving so quickly, I said. I mean, you have so many new things ahead—maybe it doesn't feel as sad for you.

Of course it feels sad, Ravi said. You guys are like family.

You just bought a home, he continued, you have each other, you're working on things. I've been rotting for such a long time.

Hey! I said. We love rotting.

It can't be all you ever do, Ravi said.

You're totally out of character, I told him. Soon you'll start therapy and decline a last round of drinks.

We'll see, Ravi said. There was no hint of a joke in his voice and that made me sad.

It was unthinkable that we might have missed something about him. That he was a stranger to us.

Ravi, I said, are you abandoning the group spirit?

Okay, Manu rushed in, let's stop feeling sorry for ourselves.

And Ravi said, Let's go find a place to eat. So that's what we did.

Life and Death

All this time, we were waiting. For the news of some momentous change; that we were being summoned to serve in real life; that the time for playing games was over. We lived with the abstract shape of the news, informing us that it had arrived. We lived with the imaginary shock. Maybe, I thought, it would also be a relief: Here it was, finally. Here was life itself.

I scanned abstractly through the list of things awaiting us, like probing an aching tooth, but I couldn't bear to think specifically about any of it.

Native Tongue

On our first morning in the apartment, we listened to the unfamiliar sounds, the layers of smells new and old. Ravi was leaving the city in two weeks. We had a lot of furniture to assemble, and all the boxes to unpack, so we stayed in bed. We lay on our backs, looking up at the ceiling and holding hands.

What are some things we love? Manu asked.

We love breakfast, I said.

And we love pastries, Manu said.

Tereza, I added.

Beers with Ravi.

And lazing about.

Having nothing to do on a weekend.

Detective mysteries. Sitting in the sun.

That's a good life, Manu said.

We continued lying in bed. Then Manu said:

Well, well.

Well, well, well, I said.

I guess it's time to get belligerent, he said.

I guess it's time to get belligerent and make a scene, I agreed.

ACKNOWLEDGMENTS

Continued thanks to my agent, Sarah Bowlin, for her encouragement and guidance.

To Callie Garnett, Sophie Missing, and the teams at Bloomsbury and Scribner for their vision, warmth, and enthusiasm.

To my first readers Maks Ovsjanikov, Vera Schoeller, Zsófia Young, Fuat Savaş, and Zach Fox for their insights and friendship.

The seed of this novel was the short story "Future Selves" published in the *New Yorker*. Although the book has diverged considerably from the story, I am grateful to Cressida Leyshon for her continued reading and discernment.

To Bryan Washington, Garth Greenwell, Katie Kitamura, and Raven Leilani for their early support and for their luminous writing.

Thank you: Maks, Zach, Anne for the joy of communion.

A NOTE ON THE AUTHOR

AYŞEGÜL SAVAŞ is the author of the acclaimed novels *Walking on the Ceiling* and *White on White*. Her work has been translated into six languages and has appeared in the *New Yorker*, the *Paris Review, Granta*, and elsewhere. She lives in Paris.